The Promise

Jessica Sorensen

For information:

http://jessicasorensensblog.blogspot.com/

Cover Photograph by Shutterstock

Cover Design by Mae I Design and Photography

www.maeidesign.com

Copyediting:

http://www.editorcassandra.com/

YA
F
SORENSON
04-08-2013

The Promise—(Fallen Star Series, Book 4)

ISBN 978-1467930574

Chapter 1
(Gemma)

I stood alone, the sky dark above me, like a rainy day, only there was no rain. The air was cold and crisp. Death was nearby; I could smell it, taste it, feel it. Through the leafless trees I spotted three figures, hovering over something with their heads bowed.

I moved for the figures, my bare feet burning against the snow. Tree branches clawed at my flesh, trying to pull me backward, warning me not to go further. But I pressed on, pushing my way there, until I stepped out into the opening.

"Hello," I called out to them, but the figures didn't turn around.

Snowflakes fell from the sky, as I inched my way closer, wondering what the figures were looking at.

"I can't believe she's gone," a girl sobbed. I knew that voice, it belonged to Aislin.

She stood between Laylen and Alex, her sobs flooding the air. My heart leapt in my chest, but not out of excitement. It leapt out of fear.

I ran for them, but a flock of crows swooped from the trees and dove for me. I ducked down, shielding my head as I shooed the crows away. But they kept swirling and diving and finally I let out a scream, which sent all of them scurrying, except for one. It hovered above whatever held their attention.

I crept closer, my heart knocking in my chest. Aislin took Laylen's hand and they turned around. Both their eyes were glistened with tears as they looked right through me and headed for the forest.

I turned back to Alex, whose head was still tipped down. "Alex," I said softly.

He dragged his fingers through his hair and let out a sigh. "Forem," he whispered the words of our Forever Blood Promise and turned to leave. His body was hunched over, head tipped down, and I wanted nothing more than to make his pain go away forever.

"Wait," I called out, reaching for him, but he was already gone.

All that was left was a hole in the ground. I stepped closer, looked down, and saw a black coffin. The lid was open. A girl lay inside, eyes shut, her skin as pale as snow, and her hands overlapped across her heart where a single red rose rested.

"No," my voice trembled as I backed away. "No, this can't be happening."

"Oh, but it is."

I bumped into something solid and I didn't have to turn around to know who it was.

I shook my head. "No, it's not."

6

A half faerie, half foreseer, and one-hundred percent dead Nicholas stepped in front of me. An evil grin spread across his face. "Yes, it is. And denial will get you nowhere." He gestured over my shoulder at the hole that held the coffin. "Look again, Gemma. Really look this time."

I shook my head again as I stepped forward and peered down into the grave. There she was again, the dead girl resting in the coffin. "It's not me," I stammered.

"Look closer," Nicholas purred.

I swallowed hard and leaned nearer. Suddenly the girl's eyes whipped open. My own purple eyes were staring back at me. "No!" I screamed.

Nicholas laughed. "Welcome to the Afterlife, Gemma. Where only the soul survives."

He shoved me forward, into the hole in the ground.

I landed in the coffin. "No!" I cried, staring up at Nicholas, the crow from the field perched on his shoulder. I started to get to my feet, but the coffin lid slipped shut, sealing me in my grave, with nothing but myself.

Forever.

Chapter 2

(Gemma)

I opened my eyes to darkness. Not a coffin, but the safety of my room. Although, I never felt safe here. The nightmare of my funeral constantly haunted my sleep. Always the same, never changing. I knew there was more meaning to it than just my death. But I had yet to discover what.

The boards on my windows blocked the outside world, but they couldn't block out the crackles of the fires and the screams that filled the air like a toxic plague, painfully reminding me of the damage I'd caused.

Since shifting the vision back, the Mark of Malefiscus had taken over the streets. Fey, vampires, and witches— and even a few Foreseers—ran wild, tormenting and killing humans.

I flipped the lamp on, climbed out of bed, and padded over to the full-length mirror. My reflection stared back at me, pale skin, violet eyes that had bags under them. My hair was pulled up into a tangled ponytail and on the back of my neck was the Foreseer's mark: a circle enclosing an "S". Just beneath it, circling my shoulder blade, was the Keeper's mark: a circle traced by fiery gold flames.

"Admiring your own reflection. How very vain of you."

I scowled at the ghost faerie, hovering over my shoulder. "I see enough of you in my dreams."

He pressed his hand over his heart, his golden eyes twinkling mischievously, just like always. "Wow Gemma, I'm honored that you think of me so often."

"Nightmares, Nicholas." I backed away through his ghostly body and climbed into bed. "Always nightmares."

"So you say." He smirked. "But I beg to differ. I think you secretly pine for me, otherwise you'd take the ring off."

I stared down at the ring wrapping my finger. My father told me it held the answers to saving the world. But all the damn thing ever did was let me see ghosts. Well, one ghost at least. A very annoying ghost.

"You know what, you have a point." I started to slip the ring off.

"Gemma," Nicholas warned. "I wouldn't if I were you."

I inched it closer to the end of my finger, intentionally taunting him. "Why? So you can continue to haunt me and drive me insane."

He shook his head and brushed his sandy hair away from his golden eyes. "I thought you understood there's more to everything than what meets the eye."

"I'll take my chances," I said and watched the ring fall off my finger and onto my bed.

The faerie was gone, evaporating right in front of my eyes like an apparition.

I let out a breath of relief and decided that from now on, I'd only put the ring on if I needed Nicholas' help, which I couldn't see happening anytime soon.

Even though it was early, I knew there was no way I'd be able to fall back asleep. So I pulled on a grey Henley and some jeans and tiptoed down stairs, the brightness of the yellow kitchen walls waking me up instantaneously. But I was surprised to find that I wasn't the only one awake at such an early hour. Laylen lay on the floor, his head tucked under the kitchen sink.

"Hey, sleeping beauty," Laylen said with a smile as he peered out. His blonde hair was damp, his long tattooed arms flexing as he twisted a wrench around a pipe. "You're up early."

"So are you." I slumped down into a kitchen chair. "What are you doing?"

"Fixing the faucet." He bashed on the pipe, "That stupid drip is driving me crazy."

"At least you can fix the problem," I muttered as I pictured picking up the wrench and banging Nicholas on the head with it over and over again.

Laylen paused. "What did you say… Gemma are you okay? You've been so down lately."

"Nothing." I shook my head, hating my downer mood. But I couldn't help it. My guilt was eating me alive. "I'm fine."

"Are you sure?" he asked. "You know you can talk to me about anything."

"I know," I replied softly, wanting to talk to him, but refusing to put my guilt on his shoulders. "It's nothing. Really. I promise."

He gave me a strange look and then leaned over the faucet, peering around the back. "I give up," he said as he stood up straight and clanked the wrench down on the counter. "I guess we're just going to have to deal with the dripping." He pulled up a chair and sat down. "Why are you up so early? Nightmares again? Or is Nicholas bothering you?"

"It's the nightmare again. I can't stop dreaming about it no matter what I do."

He frowned. "Is it still the same one?"

"It's always the same one."

We sighed at the same time. He draped an arm around my shoulder and tugged me close to him. "I won't let it happen. You're not going to die anytime soon."

I rested my head on his shoulder, wishing he was right. "Nobody can control the future." I gestured at the boarded back door. "Otherwise, stuff like that happens."

A scream rippled from outside, adding a dramatic effect to my point.

"We're going to fix it," he said, squeezing my shoulder.

I smiled, but it was a fake smile. My heart actually hurt when I thought about it. People were dead because I changed the world's future.

He dropped his hand and leaned back in his chair, nibbling at his lip ring.

"So have you ..." I fiddled with the ceramic cow in the center of the table, avoiding his gaze as thoughts of Alex swarmed my mind. The electricity was gone, but sometimes, when I thought about him, I could almost feel the sensation on my skin. "Heard anything?"

He bit at his lip and shook his head, his blue-tipped bangs falling into his eyes. "I'm sure he's fine, though. He's always been good at taking care of himself."

I never said it aloud, but sometimes I thought about going to Alex, using my extraordinary power to foresee my way to wherever he was. If I closed my eyes and pictured his face, I might be able to pull it off. But deep down I knew he left for a reason. We couldn't be together. If we were, we'd die. Still, occasionally my emotions got the best of me, and I'd stir in anger over his abandonment.

"I think we should—"

A bang on the back door cut me off. We were on our feet, the chairs tipping back and slamming against the tile. Laylen took a sharp knife out of the drawer while I hurried to the side of the back door and peeked out through a small gap in the board.

"It looks like witches," I whispered. "But I'm not one-hundred percent sure. It's too dark to get a good look at their marks."

Laylen cursed under his breath and stepped cautiously for the door, the knife gripped in his hand. "What do you think? Wait it out? Or get Aislin?"

I stared at a tall woman with wavy black hair and green eyes standing on the bottom of the back porch. Witches were the worst. Their magical powers gave them the upper hand. Unlike the vampires and faeries, they didn't even have to touch you to harm you.

The witch glanced back, flittering her eyes at a group of bodies dressed in black, her hands sparkling with purple magic.

"Go get Aislin," I ordered quickly and he took off, his feet thudding up the stairs.

It was strange calling orders. I had spent so much of my life as a nobody, and now here I was, a Keeper, preparing to take on a group of witches. *So weird.*

I searched the drawers for another knife and picked up a small but razor-sharp blade. I touched the tip with my finger. "This is all your fault," I mumbled as Laylen and Aislin came barreling down the stairs.

Aislin's golden hair was a disheveled mess, her green eyes blinking with grogginess.

"How many are there?" she asked, her voice croaking.

13

"I don't know," I said and peeked behind the board. "Five or maybe six."

She nodded and cracked her knuckles. "Who's going to open the door?"

Laylen opened his mouth, but I cut him off. "I got it." I grabbed the doorknob, my pulse erratic and my hands a little unsteady. "On the count of three ... one ... two ... three." I flung the door open, catching the witch by surprise. She jumped back, but her hands were already out, her lips uttering a chant under her breath.

I wasted no time, charging out the door and ramming my body into hers. She fell to her back and we tumbled in the cold, stinging snow, Laylen and Aislin close by. My elbow and the witch's head smacked against the ice. She let out a cackle as I slammed my fist into her face.

Another cackle and her mouth spread into a grin. "Nice try." She broke off my necklace and a purple ball of fire glowed in her hand. *"Animam tuam."* The ball lifted from her grasp and slammed into my middle.

I buckled back, trying not to panic as my stomach glowed like a night light. Aislin and Laylen had three of them down, Aislin working quickly to remove the Mark of Malefiscus from their wrists. I blinked crazily, waiting for the spell to do something. But the witches face dropped as I remained the same, unchanged, but still glowing. She gripped my arm and I pressed my fingers into her hands, digging my nails in deep.

"You're the one," she uttered under her breath, her green eyes glittering with light. "It's you."

She knew I was the star and I had to act fast. No one knew for sure what kind of connection the witches held with Stephan, but we always had to be careful. I swung back my fist, working up as much force as I could, before slamming into her head. My knuckles cracked as her eyes rolled back, her lips parting, as she slipped into unconsciousness.

I scurried to my feet, glancing around and was grateful that Aislin had gotten the marks off the others, who were wandering away, confused on how they got here. It would take a second for the spell to wear off and then they would return to their normal lives with a guilty conscience.

I dusted the snow off my clothes as I stared at the unconscious witch.

"This one knows who I am," I told them, picking up my locket.

"I'll make sure to erase her mind then," Aislin said, coming over to the witch.

I nodded, but felt guilty. I always did when it came to erasing someone's mind. Good or bad, having my own mind stolen from me gave me a soft spot for anyone else who had to endure it. But these were hard times. Drastic measures had to be taken.

The removed marks slithered away like tiny snakes. I retreated, not wanting to watch as Aislin slipped her hands inside the witch's head and extracted her memories.

Laylen followed me inside, grabbing my hand and turning me to him. "It has to be done," he said. "They can't know where you are."

I nodded. But, if I hadn't messed around with visions, then this mess wouldn't exist. I kept this to myself though, because I knew he'd try to convince me this wasn't my fault. He'd feel bad because I felt bad and I didn't want that. I wanted him to be happy.

I rubbed my stomach, which wasn't glowing anymore, but burned like I was hungry. "She threw a spell in me after she broke off my locket."

"What kind of spell?" Aislin asked as she came inside and shut the back door, locking the dead bolt and then the other three locks.

I searched my brain for the words the witch uttered. "*Animam tuam*, I think."

Aislin's eyes popped wide. "Oh... "

"What is it?" I touched my stomach again, wondering if I was going to explode or something. "What'd she do to me?"

"I don't ... It's just that ..." Her gaze was everywhere else but on me.

"Just spit it out," Laylen said sharply.

Aislin swallowed hard. "She took your life."

16

Chapter 3
(Alex)

I hated the smell of these places. Everyone smelled like they'd just rolled out of a gutter, and then dug around in a garbage can.

"You seem down, sweetie," a woman with long skinny legs said. Her blonde hair was way too thin for her round face. Her teeth were cracked and stained a yellowish-brown. She stuck her hand out, her sharp, yellow-stained nails sliding up my chest. "Maybe I can help you with that."

I pushed her back, not gently, giving her a bored expression "I'm looking for a man named Draven. Ever heard of him?"

She had, but she wasn't planning on telling me—at least she thought she wasn't. She pressed her thin lips together. "Never heard of such a man." She touched my shoulder. "Why don't you forget about this Draven?" She leaned in, putting her lips next to my ear. "I can make you forget about him. I can make you forget about everything."

I smiled maliciously and leaned toward her. "As nice as that sounds, I know what you are, so you might as well cut the crap and take me to Draven."

She moved back, still smiling. Banshees were the worst kind of faeries. Their ragged state was just an armor. Really, they were quite beautiful and alluring, except on people like me, who knew what they really were—a sign, appearing to those who were going to die soon.

"If you know what I am," she said slyly, "then you know your future is coming to an end."

"I'm not asking you about my life," I replied, unbothered. "I'm asking you to take me to Draven."

A purr vibrated from her chest and she traced her pinky nail under my chin. "What makes you think I know him?"

I clutched her wrist, squeezing tight. "My patience is wearing thin. Either you willingly take me to him or I make you take me to him."

She winced, but kept grinning. "How much is it worth to you?" She paused. "Perhaps your life?"

"My life already belongs to someone else," I said, calm and controlled, trying to push the quick thought of her out of my mind.

"Then let me be the one to collect you when you die. Let me take your soul." Her grin widened, her lips disappearing into her teeth. "When you die, make the vow that I can be the one to carry your soul to the Afterlife."

I considered this, but not for very long. "Whatever. Just take me to him."

She was pleased, ignorant of the fact that she couldn't take my soul when I died. Because it already belonged to someone else, just like I told her. And a Blood Promise was much stronger than a promise made by word of mouth.

She turned for the alley, the click of her high heels echoing up the steel buildings. As we moved, she transformed, her blonde hair thickening and curling up at the ends, her rough skin smoothing over and her teeth whitening to a shade so bright it reflected against the luminosity of the full moon.

"This way," she said and ducked behind a large dumpster where a door was hidden. She slipped a chain from her neck holding a large silver key. The key scratched inside the lock and she creaked the door open. She disappeared inside and I followed.

The air was murky and stank of pond scum. I had a hard time following her because her silhouette kept blending in and out of focus. At the end of the tunnel, lanterns lit up a room. The walls were as red as blood and there was an oval table extending down the center of the room with eight chairs encircling it. In one corner, there was a Black Angel, sleeping in a cage, her wings curled against her back. They really were sad creatures, trapped until someone freed them from their cage and wings. I remem-

19

bered the time Gemma almost let one go. Thankfully, I'd gotten to her in time.

"Have a seat," the Banshee said and exited the room through a wooden door on the left. I sat down, preparing my speech in my head, knowing if I was wrong then I'd wasted a lot of time. But part of me didn't want to be right. Part of me didn't want her to be one of them.

When the door clicked open again, the blonde Banshee returned. But she wasn't alone. A man, with dark hair, black eyes, and pale skin stood beside her. Someone who was inexperienced would probably mistake him for a vampire. But I knew better. He was more dangerous than a vampire. That's why I had my knife tucked in my jacket, within arm's reach. I was surprised the Banshee didn't pat me down back in the alley. But she probably wasn't too worried. She thought I was a normal human, sticking my nose into a world where it didn't belong.

He took a seat across from me and the space between us didn't give me much option for a surprise execution. He tapped a cigarette on the table, and then stuck it in his mouth. The Banshee woman lit it for him. After he exhaled, his eyes narrowed on me.

"So you want to talk to me about something," he said, eyes refusing to leave me.

I held his gaze, not afraid, but prepared, just like I was taught. "I need to know the location of a particular woman."

He stayed silent for a while, tapping his fingers on the table. "The Lord of the Afterlife doesn't associate with mortal women."

"I don't think she's mortal," I explained, my hand resting steady in front of me, showing him I wasn't afraid. "I think she might be one of them." I nodded my head at the blonde Banshee.

"Does she have a name?" He asked, taking another drag from his cigarette. "This woman that you seek?"

"Alana," I said, the sound of her name strangling me.

Draven motioned his hand in front of him impatiently. "Alana ..."

I felt the same lump rise in my throat when I had read it on the pages of the journal. Swallowing hard, I shoved the lump back down, burying my feelings inside. "Her name's Alana Avery."

Chapter 4

(Gemma)

"I know you're there," I said to my bedroom ceiling. "So go away."

A soft laugh. "How can you tell without the ring on?"

"Because I can hear you breathing," I said, rolling my eyes. "And I've been meaning to ask you—how can you breathe if you're dead?"

"Why do you see me if I'm dead?"

"Because I'm a freak of nature," I replied, turning onto my side. "Now go away. I'm trying to sleep."

"Oh, relax and stop feeling sorry for yourself," Nicholas' voice whispered from the corner of my room. "The witch didn't take your life."

My eyes snapped open. "How'd you know about that?"

"Because I was listening," he said with something in his voice I didn't like. "What? Did you think just because you couldn't see me that I wasn't there?"

I slowly sat up, my eyes scanning my room. "How often do you do that? Hang around and listen without me knowing."

He gave a low, devious chuckle. "Maybe you should start leaving the ring on, otherwise who knows when I'm here and when I'm not ... nice place for a Keeper's mark by the way."

I touched my shoulder blade, cringing self-consciously. "You're such a pervert." I picked the ring up off my night stand and slipped it on my middle finger.

The blonde faerie appeared, full bodied, looking like he was a living human, only he was as far from it as one could be.

He grinned. "Knew that would get to you."

"How do you know the witch didn't take my life?" I asked, getting to my feet.

He sighed tiredly. "I'm not sure I want to answer any of your questions. I'm still a little upset about you taking the ring off and leaving me in the dark by myself." He faked a pout. "It's lonely, you know."

Now I was the one sighing tiredly. "Please, just once, can you answer a question simply, without complicating things?"

His face sank into a solemn stare. It was as human as I had ever seen him look. "I will, but no more taking the ring off."

Something in his voice made me feel sorry for him, which made me feel a little bad for lying when I said, "Alright, the ring stays on. Now give me what you got."

"She can't take your life," he said, stepping in front of me. "Because your life isn't your own."

I frowned, confused. "I'm not following you."

He sat down and patted the bed, and I hesitantly took a seat next to him. "No one can just take your life. Not without taking someone else's too."

"You mean Alex's?" I hated saying his name aloud. It caused my heart to do somersaults and my eyes to sting.

He nodded. "You both have to go down together." He grinned evilly. "Which, if I'm remembering correctly, you will."

I thought about all the times one of us had almost died, but never fully sealed the deal. "Is it because of the electricity?" I asked. "Is that why we have to die together?"

"That, and the Blood Promise you both made," he explained. "You two are wound together about as tight as anyone can be. The witch might have stolen some of your life, but you'll be fine."

"So what happens if one of us actually dies?" I asked, my heart thudding in my chest. "And I mean, really dies—like forever."

"You won't," he said simply. "You both have to go down together."

Hope rose in me, but it was quickly squashed.

"Don't get too excited," he said. "You're both going to die soon. Remember the lake?"

I scowled at him for bringing up the painful vision. "Does Alex know about this?"

Nicholas shrugged. "Who knows what he's got locked away in his head. Considering the countless lies he's told, you can never really know."

"That's like the pot calling the kettle black, isn't it?"

He smirked. "Perhaps."

Normally, I would have been upset with him, but I just found out that Alex was alive. All that worrying was for nothing. But it was impossible for just one of us to make it. Either we were living and Stephan could open the portal. Or we were dead and the world was saved.

So why did my dreams say otherwise?

I went downstairs, to the kitchen and told Laylen and Aislin that everything was going to be fine. That I wasn't going to, that I couldn't, die yet.

"So Alex is okay, then?" Aislin asked, like she had been fretting he was dead, just like me.

I nodded, taking a bite of my sandwich. "At least that's what faerie boy said."

She no longer looked relieved. "But how do we know he's not just being ... well, you know, himself."

I shrugged, picking the crust off the bread. "We don't."

Laylen plopped down in a chair between Aislin and me. "I thought you were going to keep that ring off for a while, take a break from him."

"It doesn't do me any good," I said. "He can still talk to me. And his voice is the most annoying part of him. Besides, I don't feel comfortable anymore. Now that I know he can still see me, even when I can't see him."

Aislin's face fell. "Ewe," she muttered, getting my meaning. She pushed her plate away. "I think I just lost my appetite."

It took Laylen a little longer to catch on, but then he flexed his hands, irritated. "If you want, I can take care of him," he offered. "I mean, do we really need him?"

"We might." I touched the purple stone on the ring. "I mean, so far he's the only ghost I've seen, so he's got to be the key to fixing the apocalyptic mess. Besides, you can't actually touch him—his body is nothing but cold air."

He touched the ring on my finger. "Maybe I should put it on and see if I can see him?" He popped his knuckles, all tough guyish. "I could have a little talk with him."

I shook my head. "Talking with him will only make things worse."

"I almost perfected the *Scutum Distillans* spell," Aislin announced over us.

"Is that the shield lowering spell thing?" I asked.

She bit into her sandwich. "I only need one more thing and I'll have it. Then we can drop the Shield Spell from my father and attack him."

26

"What's the last thing?" I slid my empty plate out of the way.

She frowned at her sandwich and picked out a bad piece of lettuce. "More power."

"I know where you could get some." Laylen elbowed me and winked.

Abruptly, Aislin stood from the table, put her plate in the sink, and walked out silently.

"Is she still mad?" I asked. "About the … incident."

He laughed softly. "It wasn't an incident. It was an accident. And she'll get over it."

I frowned, pinching his arm. "You should be more sympathetic. Seeing us in bed like that had to be hard for her."

"Ow," he laughed, rubbing his arm. "It could have been harder. We just fell asleep together in the same bed. It was completely accidental."

I rolled my eyes. Guys were so unsympathetic sometimes. "Be nice."

"I am being nice." He pushed to his feet and gave my hair a playful tug. "That's why I'm going to go upstairs and apologize again, even though Aislin and I aren't really together."

"You could be with her," I said. "If *you* wanted to."

"I know." And then he left.

I let out a sigh and rested my head on the table. God, I had really screwed things up. Not only did I have to find a way to erase the Mark of Malefiscus mess, but I also had to prevent Alex and me from dying without the world ending. So far I had nothing but a ring that let me communicate with an extremely obnoxious faerie that apparently had been playing peeping tom on me.

It wasn't like we didn't try. We tried and tried and tried, but every path seemed to have a loophole. Change a vision—mess up the world more. Kill Stephan—the Death Walker's and Demetrius still survived. Maybe I should kill them all. But I hadn't figured out a way to do that yet. Unless somehow I could create my own deadly army.

A cool breeze blew by and a moment later, I heard heavy breathing. "Go away Nicholas," I said. "That is unless you're ready to tell me what the ring's for."

Silence was the only answer I got. I raised my head. The kitchen was empty, the back door locked, the windows still boarded. But I got to my feet and peeked in the living room. Scratching my head, I turned back. Instantly my body smacked into something—the wall. I quickly scooted away, blinking.

I wasn't alone. My hands fell to my side, my lips parting at the ghost that stood before me; dark hair, blue eyes and features similar to mine, only aged. But this couldn't be right. No, she couldn't be dead.

"Mom."

She smiled. "Hello, Gemma."

Chapter 5
(Gemma)

I shook my head, blinked my eyes, doing everything to make this horrible nightmare vanish. "You're not dead. You can't be dead."

"Gemma," my mom said, hovering before me, thin and virtually invisible. "There's no point wasting time trying to deny what's right in front of your eyes. We don't have time for that."

I was still shaking my head moronically. But I didn't care. "You can't be dead. I barely had time to know you."

"I have to be dead," she said. "Otherwise, he would have used me to get to you."

I didn't have to ask. "Stephan. He did this to you?"

She shook her head, sighing tiredly. "I did it to myself. I had to." She traced her finger along her wrist, where the Mark of Malefiscus used to be. "I had to, otherwise I'd have led Stephan straight to you." She paused. "It's always the same, Gemma. No matter what you do, I don't belong here. I was supposed to die."

I wanted to cry, bawl my eyes out until they were so swollen I couldn't see the pain. Everyone was gone. My dad. Alex. And now my mom was dead.

My hands were shaking, my stomach in knots. "How did … how did it happen?"

She pressed her lips together and headed for the table. "That doesn't matter. What matters is that I'm here to help you." She floated down in a chair, her fingers seeking the ceramic cow.

"With what? Saving the world?"

Tears stung at my eyes. I wanted to touch her, but knew it wasn't possible. The loneliness that possessed me for most of my life was resurfacing.

She placed the cow back on the table. "To help you learn what you need to do." Her gaze moved to the ring on my finger. "I'm here to help you use that."

I covered the ring with my other hand. "I don't want you to help me with that." Tears started streaming down my cheeks. "I want you to go back to your body and keep living."

"That's not possible," she said. "At least not for me."

I blinked through my tears. "Are you saying that it can be done? That someone can die, then return to their body and come back to life?"

"Yes," she replied simply, moving for my hand, but then pulling away. "If done right."

I thought about my nightmare, about the crow, the coffin and how I lay awake inside it. "Am I going to do it?"

She nodded. "You are, but it's going to be tricky."

Again, my nightmare resurfaced; Alex standing above me, fully alive, which didn't make sense. "But what about Alex? Is he going to die too?"

She shook her head. "No sweetie. He's the one who's going to bring you back."

Chapter 6
(Alex)

Underneath the light of the moon I tucked the address into my pocket and stepped out from behind the dumpster. I was still unsure how I felt about what had happened with Draven; whether I liked the answer he had gave me about my mother or what I offered up to get it.

A year of my life to the Lord of the Afterlife, which meant doing whatever he asked. What the idiot didn't realize was that my life was probably going to over before he could collect. So the joke was on him.

I stepped out into the street lined with burning buildings, ignoring the feeding vampires as I headed to my left. Each one raised their eyes at me as I passed, but they knew better than to mess with me. I knew how to kill them, unlike the many humans loitering around, which made them easy prey.

I could have stopped them, but I was in too much of a hurry to find a witch and get where I needed to go. I never considered this huge downfall when I made the decision to leave on my own. I no longer had a witch or a very talented Foreseer to make traveling easier.

Thinking of her made my pulse speed up. Growing uncomfortable with my feelings, I blinked the thought of her away, knowing if I didn't move on, I'd cave in and go back. And I couldn't do that yet. Not until I found a way to save her.

Across the street, I spotted a woman. I could tell right away, from the crescent moon and star mark she bore on her neck, that she was a witch. I crossed the street, sidestepping around an injured faerie sprawled on the asphalt, begging me to help him.

Humans weren't the only ones in danger. The faeries, vampires, and witches who didn't bear the Mark of Malefiscus were also targets, which just added more madness to the madness.

The witch saw me coming and smiled as I reached her. "Can I help you with something?" She purred, but it was threatening.

She thought I was human. I raised my shirt, showing her my left rib cage, where my Keeper's mark circled. "Still want to use that tone on me witch?" Honestly, I wasn't sure how she was going to react. If she had the Mark of Malefiscus, she'd probably try to kill me. If not, it could go either way. "I need you to perform a spell for me."

Her pale blue eyes were locked on me, assessing her options. I guessed, from the worry reflected in her eyes, that she was a normal witch. "What kind of a spell?" she asked.

"A transporting one." I stepped onto the curb, inching my way to her. "I need to get somewhere quick."

She considered my request and then the corners of her mouth quirked up. "I could do that for you," she said. "But I need something from you in return."

I sighed, shaking my head. This journey was really starting to cost me. "What do you want?"

"Your help. With removing a mark."

I gave her the strangest look. "Why would you think I could help you with that?"

"I don't think you can," she explained. "But you know someone who can."

"Someone's been removing the mark?"

She nodded, taking my arm and guiding me into the shadows of an alley, away from the dangers of listening ears. "There's a rumor that there's a Keeper that possesses Wicca powers. And she's created a spell that can remove the Mark of Evil."

Aislin. "Look," I said, prying my arm from her grip. "Even if that's true, it doesn't mean I know her."

"Then I'm afraid I can't help you." She started to leave, but I pulled her back.

"You get me to where I need to go first," I said. "And then I'll help you."

She nodded, obviously the kinder of the witch breed. "I'm Amelia," she said as I followed her inside the nearest

34

brick building, which turned out to be her house; a small space, with headless dolls, strange statues, and lots and lots of incense scattered all over the place. She locked the door behind us and went to an armoire, unlocking it with a key she retrieved from her bag. She removed a familiar black candle and purple amethyst, and sat them down on the table.

Screams rang from upstairs and my hand instinctively moved for my knife.

"My daughter, Anna," Amelia clarified, lighting the candle. "That's why I need your help. She's cursed with the mark that haunts the streets."

I dropped my hand. "Are you sure there's no way for her to escape."

"She's chained to the wall." The witch pulled out a red pill from the pocket of her black jacket.

"Really?" I frowned with annoyance. "You want me to take a *mortem pilula*."

"It assures me that you'll hold out your end of the deal," she said, urging the pill at me. "No offense, but a Keeper's word means nothing to me."

Shaking my head, I snatched the pill from her hand, realizing my little plan of screwing her over wasn't possible anymore. Well, unless I wanted to drop dead. I plopped the pill into my mouth and forced it down.

She smiled, satisfied, then gestured at the floor for me to have a seat. "Where am I taking you?" She inched the amethyst toward the flame.

"To Niveo Mountain," I replied.

She jerked the amethyst back from the flame. "Isn't that where the Keeper's Castle is?"

I shoved the candle at her, growing impatient. "Yeah, but that's not where we're going. We're going to the graveyard."

Chapter 7
(Gemma)

"Well don't I feel honored," Nicholas said from my bedroom windowsill. "A visit from two Lucas's. What's the occasion?"

"Shut up." I rushed for him, my finger waving. "You're on the crap list for keeping important things from me."

"I'm always on that list," he said, sweeping the curtain at my window. "In fact, I think I hold top slot on it."

I kept moving for the faerie, wishing I could actually get my hands on him and wring his neck. "You knew all along what I had to do. You wasted weeks of my time. And now there's hardly any time left. December 21st is almost here."

He held up his hands, grinning. "That's because you kept asking the wrong questions."

I clenched my hands. "God, I wish I could —"

"Gemma." My mother's ghostly voice shivered over my shoulder. "You need to move past this—you have more important things to do."

I dropped my hands. "How do I get to the Afterlife? You know, the land of the Lost Souls—the Afterlife where the queen reigns." I scowled at him. "There. Was that the right question?"

He clapped his hands. "Bravo, but I might add how slow you were at figuring it out."

"Answer the question," I gritted through my teeth.

His golden eyes skimmed to my mother. "Why doesn't she tell you? She's a ghost, isn't she?"

I let out a sharp choke, wanting to cry, but fought back the tears because I had a job to do. "She doesn't know how to get there. For some reason, she can't cross over. But you're a faerie—and a dead one—and that gives you a direct connection to the queen, with her being from the faerie world and all."

"Didn't I explain to you once that I'm only half-faerie." He placed his hand on his chest. "And that makes other faeries, dead or not, not very fond of me."

"Are you sure that's the real reason why," I snapped. "Because I'm sure your amazing personality helps win you fans."

He shot me a dirty look. "You know what? I really don't feel like talking to you. Not with that kind of attitude."

My fist rose. "You better tell me or I'll ..."

"Or you'll what?" He stuck out his bottom lip. "Hurt me?" An evil shadow masked his face. "Just to refresh your memory, you're not the one with the power here." He tapped his finger on his lip. "Now, perhaps if you were really, really nice to me, I might be more willing." His eyes scanned me from head-to-toe, making my skin crawl.

I opened my mouth, to spat fowl words, but a gust of wind whizzed by me. My mother ran past and straight into Nicholas. Surprisingly, she was able to grab him, her ghostly arms encircling his neck.

"You can't make me say anything," he said with a choked laugh as his body slammed into the window.

My mother's wild eyes snapped in my direction. "I'll be back in a while. Don't go anywhere."

I nodded, astonished as the two ghosts dissipated into thin air. I flopped down on my bed and let the tears pour out. My heart trembled as I mourned my dead mother. She was gone and so was my brief moment of having her.

Alone.

Always alone.

I let myself have about five minutes before I pulled it together and went to find Laylen and Aislin so I could tell them what was going on. But when I stepped into the hall, the house was as silent as a graveyard, sending a surge of fear slithering down my spine. I leaned back into my room, sneaking my knife out of the dresser drawer. Then I tiptoed down the hall, heading to Laylen's room, with the knife poised in front of me. My hand appeared steady, which made sense since I was a Keeper now. But every time I faced danger, my heart still pounded like an insane person bumping their head against a wall.

When I reach Laylen's room, my hand rested motionless on the doorknob. Hesitating, I pressed my ear to the door, but couldn't hear anything. I gently pushed it open. The room was empty. Okay, so maybe they were where Aislin slept. I started to turn, but my shoulder bumped into something solid and I jumped back, letting out a gasp. But it was Laylen.

"You scared the crap out of me." I pressed my hand to my heart.

He eyed my knife, lifting an eyebrow. "What were you doing?"

I shrugged, lowering the knife. "It seemed a little too quiet and I thought maybe something happened to you guys."

With his bright blue eyes on me, he took the knife out of my hand and tossed in on the dresser. "You're going to hurt yourself—wandering around with that."

"Hey," I said, pretending to be offended. "I'm not as klutzy as I used to be."

He didn't smile, my joke bombing big time. He backed me into the room and locked the door. The look he was giving me, for some reason, made me think of Talking Head's "Psycho Killer."

"You know, I don't think I've told you how thankful I am. How great you've been to me." He fiddled with the knife, cutting a narrow line into the top of the dresser. "You accepted me, vampire and all."

"Laylen," I said, my voice gentle. "Just because you're a vampire, doesn't mean you're bad." I placed a hand on his arm. "You're good, *you* just don't realize it."

His gaze moved to me, bright blue and beautiful. "Still … you trust me?"

"Of course I trust you," I said. "Sometimes I trust you more than anyone."

His lips slowly crept up. "I know you do." He lazily moved in front of me, running his fingers down my bare arm. "You know I never thanked you for that day in the alley, when you saved my life. Letting me bite you like that, it was really amazing."

I grew uncomfortable, remembering the bite and all the feelings that came with it. My skin warmed, my pulse quickened, and I knew he could sense it. "I couldn't let you die."

"You could have." His fingers grazed my wrist, resting on my vein. "You didn't have to let me bite you."

"Yes, I did." My voice came out squeaky.

He rubbed his lips together, continuing to touch my wrist, watching it with passion.

"Are you okay?" I asked, trying to capture his gaze. "You seem kind of …"

He met my eyes. "Kind of what?"

41

I swallowed hard, nervous energy bubbling in my chest. "Off."

Something in his expression sent a chill down my spine. "Off how?" He trailed his hand to my cheek, gently stroking my skin. "You're so beautiful."

Most girls would have been flattered. But I knew better. Something was wrong. I grabbed his hand, trying to lift it from my cheek. "Laylen ... I don't think—" He slapped his hand across my mouth.

"Stop talking." The dark shift in his eyes wound a knot in my stomach.

His fangs slid out, like murderous blood seekers, wanting to devour me. I tried to yank away, but he snatched my wrists and crashed into me. His body was ice-cold and so were his eyes. He breathed down my neck, his breath warm against my skin. "You smell so good...I just can't...can't..." Then his fangs sunk into my neck.

I struggled to get away, but he was a vampire and a Keeper and much stronger than me. He shoved me to the bed and I screamed as his fangs dipped deeper.

Chapter 8
(Alex)

So Draven wasn't lying. I'd had my doubts about the Lord of the Afterlife telling the truth. Yet, here it was—my mother's gravestone.

I left the witch, Amelia, back at the iron-barred entrance, wanting to do this alone. The graveyard was secured by a loop of trees, the leaves stained pink and orange. Her gravestone was plain, only the initials A.A. No mentioning of her being a mother, no death date. If I'd just been passing through, I never would have given the stone a second glance.

Her journals said that she worried that my father was going to kill her because she knew things she wasn't supposed to know. She also worried he would find out her secret. She had wrote that if all else failed, she would give her soul to the Afterlife, so she could one day reunite with her son and put a stop to my father's evil plan.

She had known everything. And then she had died.

I touched the rough headstone, wondering how it happened. Where was she when she breathed her last breath? If I squinted really hard, I could spot the hill that hid the Keepers castle. Anger raged in me as I stormed across the graveyard, kicking up leaves and dust. The wind howled with my anger and I knocked my fist into a tree trunk over and over again, until my knuckles bled.

"Dammit!" I kicked the tree and some of my toes crunched. I rested my head against the trunk, breathing in and out. "Come on. Get it together," I muttered, trying to calm down.

Leaves surrounded me as I pushed away from the tree and finished the walk in silence.

"Did you find what you were looking for?" Amelia asked as I came barging up to the gate.

I stopped just short of her. "I need you to take me somewhere else."

The witch's eyes narrowed. "Nuh uh. Not until you take me to the witch who can remove the mark."

"Look," I said with zero tolerance. "I'll get your daughter's mark removed, but I need to make a stop first. It's important."

She pointed her sharp fingernail at my chest. "Should I remind you about our bargain?" Her nail punctured a hole in my shirt and I smacked her hand away.

"Watch it witch," I said. "You're crossing a dangerous line."

"Am I?" She asked with a nasty grin. "Or do I need to remind you of what happens if you back out on our little bargain."

Dammit. I wanted to punch the grin off her face. I didn't have time for this. But I'd taken that stupid pill and I was going to drop dead the moment I backed out.

"Fine," I gritted through my teeth. "I'll take you to her."

When we settled in the living room of Gemma's house, my stomach dropped. It was strange, but I could sense her nearness, feel her in my veins like liquid fire.

Everything looked normal, chairs upright, TV off, photos still on the wall. They'd boarded up the windows, which was smart. I remembered when I'd heard the news from Aislin that the world had shifted into a Mark of Maleficus mess. The letter had arrived via her witch powers, which meant a small flaming ball of paper had landed on my head, torching some of my hair. I still had a tiny bald spot.

I'd read the letter, but never wrote back, not wanting the wrong person to find out where I was and come looking for me. I wanted to protect Gemma in every way possible, which meant keeping her away from me, no matter how crappy I felt about it. I deserved to feel that way though, after all the hell I'd put her through.

But now I was back in her house, about to blow everything if she found out I was here. It was strangely quiet and my Keeper instincts went on high alert. I drew out my knife, which glinted dangerously in the light of the lamp.

"What are you doing?" Amelia asked, gazing around the room. "And where's the witch? The one who can remove the mark?"

"Somewhere." I hoped, but something felt off. "Stay here a minute. I'll go get her."

Amelia sank down on the sofa, making herself at home. "Don't worry, I'm not going anywhere." She kicked her feet on the table, mud falling off her boots.

My lip twitched and my knife itched to shut her up, but I turned my back on her and headed for the stairs. Each step creaked louder and I cringed, worried Gemma might hear me. If I worked this right, I could get in and out without her noticing. But when I reached the top of the stairs and saw that her door was cracked open, I couldn't help it. It was like my legs didn't belong to me anymore; they belonged to her. By the time I reached her door, my heart was all over the place and I wanted to choke it dead for making me so weak.

I peeked my head inside, blinking against the grayness of the low light. She was inside, I could feel her slight current of static. But there was no noise. She had to be asleep.

I gently pushed the door open, knowing what I was doing was wrong, but doing it anyway. I used to be more cautious about mistakes, think things through first, but this was what she did to me. She confused my head and I ended up making stupid choices.

When I saw her lying in her bed, fast asleep, I stopped breathing. My hand fell to my side and I walked slowly across the room until I was next to her bed.

She was resting on her side, her cheek pressed against her pillow, hair all over the place, just like it always was. I should have left right then and there. I'd have been a better person if I did. But apparently, I was a selfish asshole. I let my fingers touch her hair, brushing it back and tucking it behind her ear.

She breathed deeply—soundly—not feeling the electric current. Which was strange because it was making me sweat.

I wished I could lean down and kiss her, press my lips against her cheeks. Honestly, I wished I could do a lot of things to her, things that could only be done behind closed doors. But that would never happen. Not if I couldn't stop the vision from happening the way it was supposed to.

She let out a long sigh, like she sensed I was there. I decided it was time to go. I started to turn as she rolled over on her back. And what I saw made me sick. Her hands were tied, the rope cutting into her wrists. Blood was all over her neck and shirt and it looked like ... I swept her hair back. Bite marks.

"What the?" I fell to my knees, placing my hands on her cheeks, my skin burning from her touch. "Gemma. Can you hear me?"

Her eyelids began to flutter open, but she looked like she was struggling. I pressed my hand to her cheek, her forehead, my jaw tightening. God, if he turned her I was going to kill him.

"Alex," she mumbled, her eyelids flickering open. Then she was looking at me, like she thought she was dead. Her violet eyes wide and glossed over.

"You're okay," I said, but I wasn't so sure.

Chapter 9
(Gemma)

At first I thought I was dead, that Laylen had drained all my blood and left me to rot away in my bed. That maybe Alex was a ghost, that he'd died and I'd died and we'd joined each other in death.

But then I felt the dizziness, mixed with the sparkle of electricity, and my blood soared with fire.

"You're here," I muttered like an idiot. My forever shows up and the first thing I say is "you're here." Really Gemma? I sounded like a damsel-in-distress. I moved slowly to sit and he moved back, giving me breathing room.

I raised my tied arms, touching a finger to my neck, and then winced.

"What happened?" he said, urgent and eager, just the same as when he left.

I didn't want to tell him. I knew if I did he might not think rationally and end up doing something that couldn't be erased. What Laylen did—it wasn't his fault. He was under the control of another.

"I can't remember." I played dumb.

He cut the ropes that bound my wrists and freed me. I rubbed them, trying not to think about how the ropes got there in the first place.

"Gemma," he began, trying to keep control. "Just tell me what happened."

I thought about lying again, but realized I was probably in danger and needed to get out of the house. I jumped to my feet, surprising him and my head, the room spinning with bright colors and blurry shapes.

"Easy." He wrapped his arm around my back, crossing a deadly line as he steadied me.

"Did Laylen do this to you?" he asked, like he already knew the answer.

I blinked the dizziness away. "He couldn't help it … it was the mark."

"The Mark of Malefiscus." He ran a hand through his messy dark hair, letting out a long breath. "How did he get it?" His knuckles tightened as he raised his knife, ready to stab whoever walked through the door. "Is he still here? And where's Aislin and Aleesa?"

I frowned, not wanting to be the one to break it to him. "They … umm … they all have the mark."

He was already shaking his head. "How did that happen? I thought Stephan had to put the mark on them directly. And if he was here, I'm sure you wouldn't be."

I shrugged. "I have no clue. I mean, one minute the house is quiet and the next," I gestured at my neck, feeling a lump rise in my throat. "Laylen freaked out and bit me."

His jaw went taut. "Where is he—are they still here?"

I shrugged again. "I don't know. They tied me up and the house has been quiet ever since."

A boom from downstairs sent me leaping toward him like a skittish cat. "Someone's here."

He took my hand, holding the knife out as he guided me to the stairs. We peered down, but there was only darkness.

"Stay here," he whispered, but I was already scooting past him.

"No way," I whispered. "You don't just get to show up and take over. I'm going down with you." Then I headed down the stairs, moving quietly through the dark, cupping my hand over my bleeding neck as my heart drummed in my chest.

But he beat me to the bottom, squeezing by at the very last step, giving my skin a good zap. Another bang and we tiptoed for the living room. I found myself wishing we hadn't put praesidium all around the house. Sure, it kept the Foreseers out, but it also kept this Foreseer in.

We were greeted by a woman in the living room doorway. Not just a woman, but a witch, dressed in black and hair to match. I moved to kick her and take her down, but Alex stuck his arm out, holding me back.

51

"Easy Tiger." He was trying not to smile. "This is Amelia."

My eyebrows knitted together. "You brought a witch into the house?"

"She's helping me with ... something," he said.

"Is she the witch?" Amelia stared hypnotically at my eyes.

I shook my head, rolling my eyes. "Just because I have violet eyes doesn't mean I'm a witch."

Her eyes lit up with hunger. "But you have so much power flowing off you. Both of you do."

"That's because we stuck our finger in a socket," Alex replied expressionlessly.

"Don't be cute with me little boy." Amelia narrowed her eyes, jabbing a finger at his chest. "Where's the witch? You promised me the witch that could remove the mark of evil?"

"You did *what*?" My jaw nearly hit the floor. "Why would you do that?"

Alex waved me off. "She just needs Aislin's help taking the mark off her daughter. That's all."

Amelia laughed harshly. "That's all. Do I need to remind you again what's at stake here?"

I crossed my arms and waited for Alex to explain. But, like always, he didn't.

"Look," he told Amelia. "Aislin's gone over to the Malefiscus side. She's no longer going to be able to help you."

Her eyes burnt with rage and she lifted her hands above her head, wiggling her fingers until they glistened. "Well then, I guess it's time for you to die."

My head almost snapped off as I did a double-take at Amelia. "What? You can't kill him just for that."

"We can try and find her." The nervousness in Alex's voice made my heart skip a beat. "Maybe you could use a Tracker Spell on her or something."

But Amelia only shook her head. "If that were possible, I'd have done it already. But she's off the map—no one can find her." Then without another warning, the sparks sizzled.

I let out a breath, reaching for her hands, but Alex collapsed to the floor, hitting it like a bag of bricks.

"You killed him!" I screamed, eyes wide as I stared at Alex. "You stupid witch!"

She had already moved over to the coffee table, a black candle lit, an amethyst clutched in her hand. I stormed toward her, fury sweltering like a wildfire. She must have seen it in my eyes too, because she freaked out, chanting magic words under her breath. Then she plunged the amethyst into the flame, right as I snatched hold of her sleeve. But her magic was too strong and I had to let go or be tugged away with her.

Bumping my knee on the corner of the table, I scurried back to Alex. "Please don't be dead. Please don't be dead" But he wasn't breathing and the electricity was as lifeless as the house. I sucked back tears, touching my hand to his chest, feeling for a heartbeat. "You can't be dead." Tears started to slip from my eyes. "Nicholas said you couldn't ... not without me."

But only the only answer I got was the sound of my own tears.

Chapter 10
(Alex)

I could hear her flipping out as she searched for my pulse. Sharp breathes. Humming skin. Part of me wished I was dead and this was all over. She could go on living her life, happy and free. But then, so could my father.

I forced my eyes open, meeting hers, beautiful and wildly insane. The first thing that came to my mind was to pull her down and kiss her. Which was stupid. But that was what she did to me. She made me crazy and out of control. But after a life controlled by my father, feeling insane and out-of-control was kind of a good thing.

But now wasn't the time.

"Am I dead?" I joked because it was obvious I wasn't.

Her face was pale. "No, you're not dead. You can't be dead without me."

I sat up, rubbing my head, and it felt like it'd been squeezed by vise grips. "You think that's how we're supposed to go? Together?"

She nodded. "But not because of the vision. Nicholas told me something about us."

I pulled a face at the mention of the stupid faerie. I hated Nicholas. Not just because he was obnoxious or a pain in the ass, but because of how he looked at Gemma, like he would rip her clothes off at the first chance he got. Too bad for him he was dead.

"Wait a minute!" I said. "I thought he was dead?"

"He is." She sighed, raising her hand, showing me the ring her father gave her. "I can see ghosts now. Well, just two ghost—Nicholas and my mother."

I gave her a funny look. "You're mother ... but that would mean ..."

"She died," she breathed it softly and put on a brave face I could easily see through.

I tightened my hands into fists. "My father killed her."

She shook her head, her dark hair falling in her face. "No, she did it to herself. To protect me."

I reached for her, wanting to comforter her, but she leaned back.

"Is that why you came back here?" she asked. "To find Aislin?"

I eyed her over and she squirmed. "Yeah, I needed a witch to travel so I made a bargain. I said I'd get Aislin to help her if she took me where I needed to go."

"A bargain where you had to die?" She met my eyes. "Well, that was stupid."

"Yeah, pretty stupid." My eyebrows dipped down. "But apparently I can't die? At least according to the faerie."

"He said we're a packaged deal." She pressed her lips together. "If one goes, than the other goes too."

I opened my mouth to speak, but something crashed into the front door, making the whole house rock. I was on my feet in a matter of seconds, pulling her up like she was air. "We need to go, before the wrong person shows up."

"What about Laylen?" She tugged back. "And Aislin and Aleesa."

"They're on their own now." I started for the back door, but she didn't move. She was stronger than she used to be—I could feel it through her grip. And I'd be lying if I said it didn't turn me on a little.

"But they could do things—harm others."

"I know," I said. "But what can we do? The only person I know who can remove the mark is Aislin. And if she's one of them, I don't think she's going to be very into taking off the mark."

She bit at her bottom lip and frowned. "I guess ... but my mom and Nicholas are going to be looking for me here."

"Gemma," I said, her refusal to move frustrating me. "They'll have to find us. I mean if we stay here, my father will show up. You know he will, if he's got to Aislin or Laylen."

She finally nodded. "But we have to find a way to save them, before they end up doing something they'll regret."

They probably already had, but I wasn't going to share that with her. Then she'd want to go on a saving crusade. So we disappeared into the pitch black night, fires burning in the streets, the moon a large orb that reflected against her pale skin.

"Is this far enough away?" I asked as we approached the end of the snowy driveway.

"I think so," she said and then shut her eyes. "Where should I take us?"

"A safe place." Then, even though I knew I shouldn't, I wrapped one arm around her waist pulling her close to me. Her smile murmured through me, but she pressed it back, trying to appear cool.

Then snow spun around us and she took us away.

Chapter 11
(Gemma)

I didn't know what happened. Maybe seeing him threw me off, or maybe it was what he had said about going somewhere safe that made me think of the place where my dad resided, inside his own head, where he was trapped all alone.

Alex glanced around, confused. "Where are we?"

I pulled a "whoops" face. "I think I accidently took us into my dad's head."

Alex stared at me blankly. "You took us into your dad's head?"

Things had changed since my last visit. The ocean was there, but the beach was rockier and the air was colder. The sky was full of thunder and flashes of lightening. Ocean waves crashed into the shore with the storm.

"Yeah, this is where my dad lives." How weird was this? The first time my dad and Alex meet we're inside my dad's head? I shook the absurdity away. "I wonder where he is?" I hiked up the beach, sand sneaking into my DC's. Thunder boomed above and waves threatened to steal us away.

"So this is what you thought of when I said a safe place?" Alex asked, staring at the waves.

"You know me," I joked, kicking at the sand. "I like to keep you on your toes."

He pressed back a laugh and met my eyes. "So where's your dad?"

I shrugged, puzzled. "I'm not sure. Usually he just shows up."

The corners of his mouth quirked. "Well, it's his head so he's got to be around."

I nodded, biting my lip, trying to hold back the question I was dying to ask. But it slipped out anyway. "Are you leaving again?" I sputtered.

His adam's apple bobbed. "I don't know..." He shut his eyes, breathing in the salty ocean air. "I think I should."

I wanted to argue, yell at him, beg him not to go. But I understood. I hated it, but knew it was probably the right thing to do. I nodded, voiceless.

His eyes opened, bright green, flashing against the lightening. "I don't want to."

I was startled by the rawness of his words. "Then don't."

We stared each other down, our hearts pounding faster, electricity radiating more energy than the lightning bolts. And the pounding slowed as time drifted away and our lives started to drain.

"Here," he said breaking the trance we had fallen into. He took off his jacket and slipped it on me, zipping it up tight. "Your dad might worry ... with all the blood on your neck and shirt."

I tucked my hands into the sleeves, breathing in the scent of him. "So what did you find out on your little excursion?" I asked, trying to distract my thoughts from his scent, not wanting to be a total weirdo.

We headed further down the beach. "Not much. You?"

"What do you know about the Afterlife?"

He hit an abrupt stop. "Why did you ask that?"

"Because ..." I replied. "That's where my mom said I had to go." The wind blew my hair in my face. "To visit a woman named Helena."

He shook his head, his hair stuck up in all kinds of directions. "No way. You can't go there—it's the Afterlife for God's sake, as in the place where a Lost Soul goes after someone dies an unneeded death."

I shrugged, biting at my nails. "So what? If it can fix everything then it's worth it?"

My answer seemed to make him kind of angry. "So you're okay with that—dying. And me too, since we're supposed to be a package deal."

I placed my hands on his shoulders and he flinched. "You're going to be fine. You're going to bring me back."

"No freaking way," he snapped, moving his face closer to mine. "It should be me. You don't need to die."

I started to argue, but was cut off by the sound of a familiar voice.

"Gemma."

Dropping my hands from Alex, I turned to my dad, giving him a small smile. But he looked anything but happy to see me, his violet eyes unwelcoming, his silver robe blowing in the wind. "You need to go, now!"

I jolted my head back, shocked. "What's—"

A crackle of ice interjected and the rushing water rapidly froze over, the waves chilling in their place. Suddenly black-cloaked figures with corpse-like skin marched toward us, stirring up a cloud of sand.

The Death Walkers had returned.

Chapter 12
(Alex)

She made me so angry sometimes. As she stood there, telling me she was going to die so she could go to the Afterlife, I wanted to trap her in my arms and lock her away until this was all over. Obviously, I couldn't. But I really considered it. Her casual attitude toward her own life was driving me insane. I wished she could see what she really was—what others saw.

I remembered the first time I saw her at school, walking across the parking lot. She was so innocent and confused and beautiful. I almost jumped back in my car and drove home. Sometimes I wished I'd gone through with it. Instead I toughed it out, being a total dick to her, watching her hurt with every rude word I uttered.

Still, she forgave me. Well, eventually... kind of. There were times, when I realized what was at stake, that I wanted her to hate me. It'd have made things easier if she refused to let me touch her and want her in the forbidden way that I did.

I was just about to start tearing into her, banning her from going anywhere near the Afterlife, when her dad showed up out of nowhere, screaming at her like a mad man. I was confused until I saw the Death Walkers planting their ice where it didn't belong.

With one swift movement, I slid my hand into hers and sprinted down the beach, putting as much distance between her and them as I could. But she slipped on the ice, taking out our balances with her. She landed on her back, cracking her head against the ice and I fell on top of her, my body pressing into hers.

She blinked over at the ice and then back at me. "Hold on," she whispered, enclosing her arms around my neck and drawing me close to her.

The electricity poured through us, melting the ice below our bodies. Her hair blew in my face, her eyes shut and all I could think was take me now, because it really seemed like the perfect time to die.

There was a flash and the next thing I knew we were falling to another world.

When the movement stopped I was shocked.

I never thought I would see this place again. I didn't want to see it again. It reminded me of everything bad and everything we needed to fix. We were in the mountains, where the piece of the star crashed to earth.

"This is what you were thinking of?" I asked. "In the middle of all that chaos."

She shrugged, an awkward shrug because I was still lying on top of her. "Why would anyone come looking for us up here?"

"Yeah," I said, pushing to my feet. "But we're going to end up freezing to death." I cocked an eyebrow at her. "And I thought you hated the snow." I pulled her to her feet, brushing the snow from her head and I felt her shiver from my touch.

"I'm getting used to it, I guess." But she pulled a face as she said it and I had to hold back a laugh. She looked at me, her eyebrows dipping together. "Won't you freeze?" She fumbled to take my jacket off her.

But I fastened the zipper back up. "Keep it on," I said, tugging the hood over her head. "I'll be fine."

She eyed my short-sleeve shirt. "Are you sure be-cause—"

I cut her off—there was no way I was going to let her take that jacket off. "I wonder how they ended up in your dad's head."

She fiddled with the zipper. "Do you think ... do you think he'll be okay with them in there?"

I nodded, even though I had no idea. "He's in his own head, which means his real body is somewhere else, so I think he's safe." I paused, staring out at the snowy mountains. "We need a plan."

"We have a plan. We're going to find my mom." She leaned back against a tree, snow drifting down from the branches. "She's getting the information from Nicholas. She's probably waiting for me back at the house."

"Info about how to get into the Afterlife?" I asked, tracing the tip of my shoe against the spot where the snow always melted—the spot where the star hit.

She got this really funny look on her face, like she was trying to see into my head or something. "Do you know how to get there?"

"No," I lied casually. There was no way I was going to offer up information that would get her killed. "I have no idea."

She frowned, like she was on to me. Then she moved away from the tree and stood in front of me, crossing her arms, attempting to act tough. "Is that the truth?"

"Yeah." I hated lying to her, but hated the idea of her dying more.

She didn't believe me. "I need to find my mom."

"Are you ... are you doing okay with that?"

She nodded, but the electricity shot up a level and I was pretty sure she was about to cry. I opened my arms to hug her, but then pulled back, pretending to have an itch on my arm. Lost in her thoughts, she didn't even seem to notice. Then her gaze darted to the side, and she let out a heavy sigh. "How did you find me?" she asked nervously.

Now I was the one growing nervous, because there was no one there.

Chapter 13
(Gemma)

He probably thought I was insane, standing there, talking to myself. But I was talking to the blonde faerie with the irritating voice. A.k.a Nicholas, the faerie/Foreseer.

"How'd you find me?" I asked, trying to ignore the chill he brought with him. I sensed Alex tense. "It's Nicholas," I explained.

"And your mom?" He asked and I shook my head.

"Where is she?" I patted my pockets, hunting for a knife I didn't have.

"She's been detained." His golden eyes sparkled against the faint sunlight shadowed by clouds. "But don't worry, I'm here to help you."

"Sure you are." I rolled my eyes. "Because we all know that's your number one goal in life."

"Oh Gemma," he said overdramatically. "Your distrust hurts me so much there aren't even words to express how I feel."

"Go away," I mumbled and Alex gave me this perplexed look. "And don't come back until you're with my mom."

"But I'm here to help," he said, crossing his heart. "I promise."

Alex trampled beside me. "What's he saying?"

Nicholas grinned and waved his hand in front of Alex's face. "God, I hate you." His hand moved for Alex's hair, not quite touching it. "And that stupid hair."

"He's saying he's a moron." I glared at Nicholas. "And I like his hair."

"What?" Alex said, fixing his hair.

"Nothing." I pointed my finger at Nicholas. "Either tell me what to do or move on."

"Fine. My word, no sense of humor." He sighed. "You need to come with me."

"I can't do that," I said. "You're dead."

"And you'll soon be too," he said. "Once you pick the way you want to die. Now, I'd probably pick something poetic, like poison from a vile. But you—"

"Pick the way I want to die!" I shouted over him, sending snow from the branches. I lowered my voice. "I'm sorry, but what?"

Alex was tugging on my hand, trying to get me to turn to him, desperate to know what was going on.

"Just a second," I held up a finger, keeping my eyes on Nicholas. "Start explaining from the beginning."

He yawned, feigning fatigue. "It's kind of a long story."

"Then give me the short version, just don't leave out anything important."

He sank down on a rock, folding his arms. "Once upon a time there was a beautiful princess," he started and I shot him a glare. "You asked for the short version and I'm giving it to you—this is how it starts."

I sighed and sat down on another rock, patting the spot next to me.

"What are we doing?" Alex asked, putting space between us as he sat down.

"We're listening to a story," I said. "Or at least I am."

"Like I was saying," Nicholas continued, annoyed. "There was a beautiful princess, who was more extraordinary than any other princess because she liked to help the world. The problem was she wasn't very good at helping. Every time she fixed a problem, she caused another. Until one day she caused a problem so great, it cost the lives of many innocent people."

I gulped and Alex whispered in my ear, "What's he saying?"

"I'll tell you when he's finished." I motioned at Nicholas to continue. "Go on."

"What the princess needed to realize was that to fix the problems she'd caused, she needed to save the Lost Souls of the innocent lives that were taken."

"And how do I save these Lost Souls?" I asked, already knowing his answer, but wanting him to say it anyway.

"By going to the Afterlife and bargaining with the queen for their release."

I frowned, remembering the last queen—The Queen of the underworld. "A queen? The one my mother was telling me about?"

He smirked. "Queen Helena."

"And what's this queen like?" I asked. "Is she as bad as The Queen of The Underworld?"

"No, she's much worse than the Queen of The Underworld." He grinned, amused with himself.

"So how do I get her to free these souls?" I asked. "If she's that bad? And how do I even get to the Afterlife to begin with?"

"You get help from a Banshee," he said simply.

I gaped at him. "What the heck's a Banshee?"

"It's a woman spirit whose cry signals death," Alex explained, dusting the snow from the rock. "She's also the one who carries the Lost Souls to the queen."

I let out a long breath. "So we have to find a Banshee who will help us."

Alex's forehead creased. "Why?"

I sighed and quickly explained everything Nicholas had told me.

"So do you know any Banshee's hanging around who might be nice enough to help us out?" I asked, hopeful, but knowing the chances were low.

"Actually I do." Snow began to flutter from the sky as he stood up. "My mother."

My head whipped in his direction and I almost fell off the rock. "Your mother's a Banshee? How did you ...what?"

Nicholas let out a snort. "Oh, this is so comical."

"There nothing funny about his mom being dead," I snapped.

"Oh, I'm not laughing because his mother's dead," he replied, still grinning. "I'm laughing because she's a Banshee."

I shrugged. "So?"

"A Banshee is of the faerie realm," Alex said, as if he knew exactly what the argument was about.

My expression fell. "Oh." I paused. "How did that happen?"

He shrugged, kicking at the snow. "Those journals I found that night we snuck into my house, well, they talked about her dying—that she feared my father was going to kill her. And that he would learn her secrets. But then she wrote she'd find a way to cross into the Afterlife and become one of the queens Soul Collectors, also known as a Banshee. That way she could still have a connection to earth and help us when the time was right. So I started

71

poking around, asking some people and I found out its true. She's a Banshee."

There was so much sadness in his eyes, even though he was trying to conceal it. I couldn't help myself. I wanted to kiss away his pain, so I did. A bold move for me, but hey, it had to happen eventually.

He looked surprised and I started to jerk back, because really, it was a stupid thing to do—I mean, at any moment, he and I could drop dead from the intoxication of the electric connection we shared.

But he refused to let go, pressing me closer, tasting me, feeling me, wanting me. So I let myself get carried away for a second, not caring about the star, or the world, or the fact that Nicholas was watching us like a weirdo.

Finally, it became too much and we broke away, gasping for air, eyes untamed, wanting something we could never completely have. The ice on the trees dripped, making the snow under our feet a murky puddle.

"I think I'm going to throw up," Nicholas mumbled.

"Then throw up." I raised my eyebrows at him. "If it was that bad to watch then you should have turned your head."

He pulled a face. "Then you should have turned your head," he mimicked with exaggeration.

Alex turned toward where he guessed Nicholas to be. "Hey, I got an idea, why don't you shut it."

I nodded my head discretely, mouthing: *behind you.*

72

Alex shook his head, irritated, and then reached into his pocket. "This guy named Draven, who's the Lord of the Afterlife, gave me this address. Supposedly, it's where my mom is."

I took the paper from him and unfolded it. "Reykjavik?" My eyes elevated to him, wide and shocked. "Iceland. Your mother's in Iceland. God, it's good the snow's starting to grow on me."

"Actually it's colder here than it is there," he explained.

"Oh." I folded the paper back up and handed it to him. "Okay, it's good you got an address and everything, but how are we supposed to get to Iceland?"

He cracked his knuckles, a deep thought masking his face. "Your Foreseeing thing only works if you've seen the place, so maybe if you had a mental picture of how it looked, we could get there."

"But where does the mental picture come from?" I asked. "Because all I see when I think of Iceland is a big chunk of ice."

He contemplated this. "Maybe if we had a picture you could look at."

"Where are we going to find one of those? The internet doesn't work at the house."

"We wouldn't go to the house. It's too dangerous."

"What about the library?" Nicholas interrupted, stepping between us.

I stared at him strangely. "Did you just offer up something useful on your own?"

He shrugged. "There's a first for everything."

"What's he saying?" Alex asked, his eyes searching desperately to see him.

"He said we should try the library ..." I trailed off as Nicholas strolled away whistling. "I haven't been to town since all hell broke loose, so I'm not sure if anyone's still running things like libraries. Although, Laylen picked up groceries from somewhere."

His eyes flitted to my neck, and I knew he was thinking about the bite. "Well, we could try it ... carefully." Then he pointed a finger at me. "And I'm stressing the careful part."

I extended my hand, ready to take us to town. But then I stopped and turned to Nicholas. "What happens after I free the Lost Souls?"

"Then you go to the lake and sacrifice your life, just like you're supposed to," he said honestly.

My hand remained suspended in midair, my jaw slack.

"What'd he say?" Alex asked. "Probably nothing that has any truth to it."

I blinked until I saw spots, and then looked at him. "He said he'd tell us when we get that far."

He pressed his lips together as I reached for his hand, electricity surging from the contact, and I shut my eyes and swept us away back to Afton.

Chapter 14
(Alex)

I could tell she was lying. Whatever Nicholas said to her was bad. But she wasn't ready to tell me yet.

When we landed again, we were tucked away in the alley that lined the back entrance of the library. Snow was falling from the sky, making everything a sheet of slippery white. I ran my hand across the hood covering her head, sweeping away the snowflakes. Then we hurried to the back door. There were no windows close, so I couldn't see what was going on inside.

"You think it's open?" she asked, bouncing up and down from the cold.

I shrugged, grasping the handle on the door. But it was locked. Of course.

"You're skins turning blue." Her violet eyes widened as she looked at me.

"I'm just a little cold," I said and when she reached for the zipper of the jacket, I trapped her hand. "I'm not going to take it back. I'm fine. I promise."

She got this weird look on her face and then she enclosed her hands around my wrists, her pulse slamming against her fingertips. She bit her lip as she rubbed her hands up and down my arms, creating friction, electricity, warmth.

"Better?" she asked after she'd finished.

"Sure." My voice cracked and I rolled my eyes at myself for showing how weak her touch made me. My gaze skimmed her from head-to-toe. "What about you?" I raised my eyebrow at her, giving her a look that made her hide a blush.

"You need me to warm you up?"

She shook her head and I turned for the entrance door, smiling at myself.

The front door ended up being locked too, even after I kicked it and shook the living daylights out of it.

She let her head fall against the wall. "Now what?"

"I don't know." I glanced next door at the open restaurant behind us. I guess people had to eat. "Think they'd have a computer we could use?"

She shook her head. "Doubtful. Maybe we should just break the window."

"The alarm would go off and draw too much attention." Across the street, there were only houses and many of them looked as dead as a graveyard. But a few streets back, I could see the pointed roof of the school. "I think I have an idea."

***

She was fidgeting anxiously with everything she could get her hands on. "I can't believe it's still going—you'd think they'd cancel it or something."

"I'm pretty sure hell could freeze over and school would still be mandatory." I yanked the heavy glass door open, letting her walk in. "Hey, this is where we first met."

"Yeah …" She bit at her nails.

"You know, I didn't really feel the way I acted that day," I dared utter the dangerous words.

She nodded, still preoccupied with the hall where people moved to and from class.

"They won't even notice we're here," I said, trying to calm her down, because her jittering was rubbing off on me a little. "And if they do, they'll think we're new students or something."

"I know," she muttered and started down the hall, with her head down.

I suddenly realized what the problem was. She wasn't scared of being caught. She was scared off being here, in the halls that had tormented her for almost four years.

I wasn't sure what to say to her—really I didn't think there were any words that could take her ache away. So I did the only think I could think to do. I took her hand, entwining our fingers together. Her pulse was racing, but not from my touch. She clutched on, not wanting to let go.

But eventually, we would have to.

"So this is what Iceland looks like?" She frowned at the computer screen. "I thought you said it wasn't cold there."

"No, I said it wasn't as cold." I tapped my finger at the screen. "There's still snow."

She tilted her head to the side, examining the photo. "What do you think that little roads for?"

"I don't know, but this is the best picture I could find," I told her, "Plus there's a lot of bare space around, so we don't have to worry about anyone seeing us appear out of thin air."

"And then what? We just roam around until we find the address? The place looks pretty big."

"We'll get a taxi or something."

"Seems kind of amateur." She pouted.

"Don't worry." I gave her hair a playful tug. "I'm sure there'll be plenty of times where we'll need your wonderful Foreseer power."

"Yeah, I guess." She clicked the mouse on the print page button and then rolled back the chair to stand. As she waited impatiently for the printer to screen out the picture, I spotted the figure of a vaguely familiar blonde-haired girl walking toward me. Kelsey something or another. Really, I didn't get it. I didn't know if it was just a girl thing or what, but she really seemed determined to make Gemma's life a living hell.

"Oh my God," she exclaimed, springing up and down on her toes.

I turned my back on her, taking Gemma's arm, and whispering, "Code red."

She stared at me like I was a lunatic.

Shaking my head, I snatched the picture from the printer and dashed for the door, towing her along with me.

"What are you doing?" She worked to keep up with me.

"We've been spotted," I hissed, not wanting to draw attention.

Her violet eyes skimmed the room and then her lip twitched. I heard Kelsey yammering something, but I was already swinging through the door. Gemma didn't follow. She froze in the doorway.

"What are you doing?" I asked, but she only stared straight ahead at the wall. Kelsey jaunted up, an evil look on her face as she narrowed her eyes at Gemma.

"Well look who—"

Gemma let the door swing shut right in her face, her nose smashing into the glass.

"Ready to go?" she asked, grazing past me as if nothing had happened.

"Yeah," I said with surprise. "Let's go to Iceland."

Chapter 15

(Gemma)

It might have been a childish thing to do. Letting the glass door hit her in the face like that, but I just wanted one moment to cause her as much pain as she caused me, during my four years of High School hell.

Of course hers ended up being physical pain, not emotional. But I was okay with that.

I studied the photo of Iceland as we made our way around the back of the school where some of the stoners liked to hide out and smoke. But it wasn't break time, so I knew it would be vacant. Out of the view of the school yard and windows, I knew it would be safe.

But when I ducked behind the garbage can, I was caught off guard by a vampire feeding ... "Mr. Sterling?"

Alex and I exchanged baffled looks and then Alex swiped a stick from the ground. The woman vampire with auburn hair, dark skin, and a triangle mark on her neck—the Mark of Malefiscus—kept draining the blood from my

old astronomy teacher's neck. Alex prowled like a preda-
tor behind her and with one quick motion, rammed the
stick through the vampire's chest. Her perfect body exploded into ashes, blackening the snow where she once
stood.

From behind his glasses, Mr. Sterling's large eyes
blinked uncontrollably. "What happened ... I don't ..." He
cupped his hand around his bleeding neck and Alex guided him away from the garbage can.

"Go inside and tell the nurse you were cut," he instructed.

Mr. Sterling nodded, bewildered as he staggered for
the back door of the school.

"Ready?" Alex asked, eager not to waste more time.

I held the picture in one hand and Alex's hand in the
other. I took in the snow lining the grass, the water, the
shallow hills, feeling myself there. And when I opened my
eyes, I was standing in the picture, only we were on a
road.

"Son of a—" Alex cursed as the nose of an airplane
dipped for us. We ran, tripping across the ice, and barely
missed getting taken out by a plane. We didn't stop running until we reached the fence, the top trimmed with
barbed wire.

"How do we get over?" I asked, clutching onto the
metal links

Alex's eyes searched for an escape route, while my
gaze fixated on what was beyond the side of the fence. A

81

parking lot, packed with cars. And there was one—a bright red one—that I focused on. I slid my hand onto his arm and felt the zap as I foresaw us over to the red car.

"Well, I guess that's one way to do it." He tried not to smile, but the corners of his mouth threatened upward.

"So what's next?"

"A taxi." He weaved thru the parking lot, his shoes crunching in the snow. I scurried after him, struggling to keep up. You know, it was confusing how this Keeper's thing worked. When I was fighting, I could be graceful. Yet, here I was walking across the snow, and my feet didn't want to stay under me.

The entrance doors glided open and we began our search for a payphone. But finally we gave up and Alex asked a security guard if there was a phone we could use. He must have thought we were a couple of homeless people, with the dirty look he gave us.

Thankfully, he spoke English and directed us to a phone booth, where I watched people scurry back and forth for the terminals, wondering if any of them were faeries, witches, or vampires in disguise.

He hung up the phone. "Taxi's on its way."

We found an empty seat and waited for the taxi to show up. Alex was jiggling his knee up and down, nervous energy effervescing through him. My skin grew hotter and I started to sweat underneath the jacket

"So are we going to ever split up again," I asked, throwing him off guard.

He deliberated his answer gravely. "Honestly, it'd probably be better if we did."

I nodded, agreeing, yet not agreeing. "Okay. But when?"

"Since we're here ..." His eyebrow arched. "We could just wait it out and if things get too bad, then we'll promise to go our separate ways."

I let out a soft laugh as I turned my hand over, tracing the scar of our forever promise. "Is this just a verbal promise or do we have to cut our hands again?"

Hesitantly, he took my hand, dragging his thumb down the scar. He brought my palm to his lips and brushed it with a kiss. Then he returned it to my lap and said nothing more.

I wondered how long we were going to survive each other.

The taxi ride was a long one. The air smelled of old cheese and sweaty socks, and I had to hold my breath most of the way. But that was only part of the problem. Somehow I'd forgotten how hot and intense it was when Alex and I were squished in a car together. It was like a lightning storm had erupted in a confined space, the air static charged. At least when we kissed it was a quick rush of energy, but this ... it was going to be the death of us if we didn't arrive at our destination soon.

Just when I was thinking I was going to pass out, the taxi pulled up to the curb. The slightly tilted street was outlined with two-story houses compacted together, the lamp posts illuminating the snow flurrying down from the sky. We hopped out, Alex paying the driver before he sped off.

"Which one is it?" I asked.

Alex slid the paper out of his pocket. Then he walked up the street, glancing at each house, finally coming to a stop in front of a white one with a green roof and snow-coated shrubbery trimming the yard. "I think this is it." He returned the paper to his pocket and swung the gate open. We walked up to the front door, my eyes wandering up the quiet street.

"Are we safe?" I asked.

"Are we ever safe?" He knocked on the door.

The only answer we got was an echo. After pounding on the door two more times, he went for the doorknob, but I swatted his hand away.

His green eyes sparkled like emeralds as he stared at me with an amused look. "Is something wrong?"

"It just seems like every time this happens—every time someone doesn't answer the door—it ends badly. Like we get chased down by a crazy witch or something," I said, remembering Aislin and mine's little journey and how it ended with a witch and her store burning down.

"You want to wait out here, while I go in and check things out?" he asked.

"No, I don't want anyone to go in. I want the door to open and your mother to be standing there, looking happy to see you."

His mouth sunk to a frown. "Yeah, I don't think that's going to happen."

"I know." I sighed. "But it'd be so nice, if just once, something was that easy."

But I knew better. He knew better. And he didn't say anything else. He took out his knife and creaked the door open. "Stay behind me," he whispered as we crept inside.

The house was bare, the walls scorched with residue from an old fire. I wiped my hand along the burnt wallpaper and rubbed my fingers together. "It's ash," I said, wiping my hands on my jeans.

He looked perplexed. "It's weird, like it burnt on the inside but not on the outside."

We stared at each other and flinched as a wail resonated through the empty house.

"What was that," I hissed.

He swallowed hard. "I think it's my mother."

Chapter 16
(Alex)

It was a sound that put hairs on end, raised bodies from the grave, warned people of their impending death. This was the second time I had heard a Banshee's cry and I wondered if each one shaved more and more time off my life.

I kept my knife out because I wasn't sure how she would be. Would she appear in her hag form? Or look like herself?

I heard the thumping of her footsteps coming down the stairs, and I shifted to the side, putting myself between Gemma and the stairway, just in case. When I saw the figure, long brown hair, bright green eyes, I guessed it was her. But the similarity in our eyes was so striking that I swear hers had to be fake—an illusion of my own mind.

Her hand trailed along the railing until she reached the bottom of the stairs. At first she looked angry, like I was nothing more than an intruder. But then she smiled, her lips opening to speak.

But the sound of her voice was nothing but a screech. Gemma and I flung our hands over our ears as my mother shook her head.

"Sorry." Her voice was angelic. She motioned for us to put down our hands. "It's a habit," she explained.

I nodded and then she was hugging me tightly like I was still a child.

"You're so grown up. I can't believe it."

Then her gaze darted over my shoulder, eyes lighting up. "And who's this?" But she grew quiet, undoubtedly catching sight of Gemma's eyes. It was always her eyes that gave her away. They were hauntingly beautiful.

"Oh my." My mother opened her arms, leaning in to give Gemma a hug. Gemma looked uncomfortable with the situation. Her broken, emotionless, parentless past made her uneasy with affection. "I can't believe you made it through. Although, with all the madness going on, I highly doubt it's over yet."

"You know about the mark?" I asked and then shook my head. "Of course you do. You're a ... faerie." Something occurred to me at that moment. What if she had the mark?

But it was like she could read my mind. She rolled up her sleeves and lifted her hair away from her neck. "All mark free. Even my Keeper's mark's gone now that I've died."

87

"You're lucky," I muttered.

She frowned at me. "You need that for now. It'll help you stay alive."

She was right, but it didn't mean I liked it. "So we need your help with something," I said, wanting to talk to her more, but knowing I was running out of time.

"I know you do," she said. "I've been waiting for you to show up."

My grip constricted on my knife. "Then why didn't you come looking for me."

"I can't leave this place," she said, with sadness in her voice. "This is the place I was assigned to watch over."

"So how are you going to help us?" I asked. "If you're stuck here?"

"I'll help you escape from here."

I gazed around at the charcoal building. "Did this place burn down once?"

"No, this is death." She said it matter-of-factly. "So I'm guessing you need to get to the Afterlife to see the queen."

I nodded. "That would be the problem."

"Well, it's not going to be easy." She sat down on the bottom step. "There are certain things required to enter the land of the dead without actually being dead."

"What kind of things?" Gemma asked and I got the impression she already understood that these things were probably bad.

"The first thing," my mother eyed her ring, "you already have."

Gemma twisted the ring. "And the second?"

"Is looking like you're dead," she said lightly.

Gemma winced. "Look like I'm dead."

"Okay, how do we make it look like *I'm* dead?" I asked.

"Not you sweetie." Her eyes settled on Gemma. "Her."

"No freaking way." My voice came out composed, but on the inside I felt like I'd swallowed a jar of needles.

"It has to be me," Gemma said, just like she always did. In her eyes this was all her fault, even if she was trying to fix a mess my father and her father created.

"You don't know that." I stepped in front of her. "You just always assume it has to be you."

She shook her head, her hair going everywhere and I had to stop myself from brushing it back. "No, I've seen it. I'm dead in a coffin and Nicholas is waiting for me."

"How long have you been hiding this?" I rubbed my hands across my face, wanting to yell at her and at the same time kiss her. I flexed my hands a few times, choking back the anger bursting in me. "Well, that still doesn't mean it has to be you."

"Yes it does," my mother and her both said at the same time.

My mother stood to her feet, giving me a sympathetic look. "She has the ring, she has the ghost connection, and she's the one who shifted the vision that led to this." I started to speak, but she talked over me. "Now, I know it's not fair—I know it's not her fault. But that's the way things are—how life, works."

"Okay, so what do I need to do?" Gemma asked. "I mean, how do I look dead?"

"This is a stupid idea," I interrupted, but they both blew me off.

"You'll need to have a funeral. Helena needs to think you're dead."

Gemma was nodding, like this plan didn't bother her at all. "Okay, I can do that."

"We need a different plan," I said loudly. "One where she doesn't have to die."

"And we need a witch," my mother kept going. "One that we can trust." She turned to me, hopeful.

"Aislin's marked, if that's what you're getting at," I said flatly. "She can't help us."

"I might know someone. I'll be right back." Then she left, hurrying up the stairs.

I shook my head, irritated, and not understanding why it had to be Gemma, or why my mom was so determined it had to be done this way. I turned to Gemma, watching her squirm, trying to pretend she was calm.

"Stop looking at me like that," she said, tucking a strand of hair behind her ear. "It has to be me. It always had to be me."

"No, it doesn't." I kept looking at her, letting the electricity get to her, hoping she'd lose focus of her sacrificial plan. "Give me the ring and let me do it."

She hid her hand behind her back, as if I couldn't just reach over and take it.

"Gemma, stop being stubborn."

She looked infuriated. "I thought we'd gotten passed all this. That you understood I needed to make my own decisions."

"This is different. This is death." I turned her so we were face-to-face. "Please don't do it."

"I'll come back," she said, her voice softening. "I can't die completely. Not without you."

Losing my cool, I slammed my fist into the wall. "Gemma, I swear to God, would you please just—"

"Alright," my mother announced as she whisked down the stairs. "My witch is on board, but you two are going to have to go to her place and pick it up."

"Pick up what?"

She neared the bottom step, the light of the moon shining through the window and for a second she looked like someone else, like someone I once saw. It was like she'd momentarily shifted out of focus, revealing her true identity.

When I blinked, she shifted back.

She was smiling. "The poison that will kill Gemma," she replied calmly.

Chapter 17
(Gemma)

I wasn't going to play courageous and pretend that I wasn't scared out of my mind. The very idea of dying was enough, but adding poison to the mix had my heart racing a million times faster. But I couldn't let him know. I had to play it cool, because he was freaking out. In fact, ever since his mother had made the announcement about the poison, he seemed a little off, walking silently with his eyebrows knitted together.

His mother gave him an address and sent us on our way. The house she was in had some sort of entrapment on it and she could only leave to collect souls. So it was just the two of us, which didn't seem so bad at the moment.

We walked the snowy streets, underneath the light of the lampposts, snow falling, the silent air kissing our cheeks.

"Why do you think it's so quiet here?" I asked as we turned a sharp right and headed down a road that sloped to a cluster of dark houses.

"I'm not sure." He tucked his hands in his jean pockets. "But I don't like it. It's too quiet."

"It is," I agreed, watchfully peering at the houses settled with darkness. I wondered what was hiding in them. Were they watching us? "It's just so different. I mean, in Afton there were vampire and faeries and witches everywhere. And here it's just dead. Everything in the airport seemed normal."

"They might have been in disguise or something … or maybe we weren't looking hard enough." He trailed off like he just realized something. "Or maybe …" Then he snatched my hand and rushed us to the side of the street, running like a mad man. "We have to leave. Now."

I stumbled to keep up with him and bumped my knee into a garbage can. "Why? What's wrong?"

But he kept sprinting and dove behind a small brick house, hiding us in the shadows.

"What's wrong?" I hissed as he extracted his knife.

"Gemma take us away from here," he snapped, pacing left and right. "Now. We need to go."

But I shook my head. "Not until you tell me why you're flipping out. Is this because of the poison? Because I'm going to do it—you can't stop me."

"No, it's because that wasn't my mom," he bit through his teeth furiously and kicked the wall of the house.

"But you—"

He covered my mouth. "Don't you think it's strange? I mean, it was all so easy. We just walked up and there she was with all the information. And a plan."

I waited for him to remove his hand. "It's strange, but I think you're overreacting."

"When the Banshee was coming downstairs," he explained quickly. "I thought she looked like someone else— but I couldn't place who. I just realized who it was. It was the Banshee I met when I got the address for this place."

"Okay... "I pressed my back against the house, blending into the shadows the best I could. "But why does that matter? I mean, she looked like your mom, didn't she?"

"Yeah, but Banshees can change their looks," he said. "They can transform into someone else."

"So you don't think that was your mother?" I asked. "But why would another Banshee do that? It doesn't make sense."

"I'm not sure." He lightly touched my arm. "But I think we need to leave until we know for sure. We can't just go back and hope I'm not right. That'd be stupid."

I wasn't sure if he was being honest, or just trying to stop me from taking the poison. "I think we should—"

Nearby, a set of garbage cans tumble over, rattling the air. A dog howled at the moon, bright and full, causing a sputter of dogs to join in. We flinched and Alex whirled, knife swinging, ready to kill anyone who ventured to move in on us.

"Well, look at you two. Hiding out, like two frightened little kids." Laylen's tall, pale silhouette slid out from the shadows and into the light of the porch.

"Son of a," Alex muttered, aiming the knife at Laylen.

A grin crept up on Laylen's face as he showed us his fangs. "I thought you'd be happy. I'm finally what you always saw me as—a killer."

Alex began to speak, but a voice rose above his.

"Maybe he always saw you for what you were supposed to be." Aislin appeared out of nowhere, golden hair sparkling in the moonlight. An eerie grin strained at her lips as she stroked Laylen's shoulder. "What we were both supposed to be."

Their forearms were marked with a triangle outlining a red, Greek-like symbol—the Mark of Malefiscus. It stained their hands red and made them grin in a way that shot a shiver down my spine.

"Get us out of here," Alex hissed, but I couldn't seem to take my eyes off them. They were evil now and I knew they would hurt us. And where was Aleesa? She was marked too, the last time I'd seen her. Had they lost her?

"She's fixated by me," Laylen said, sweeping his hair back. "She's remembering the bite—and how good it felt."

I touch my neck, memories iridescent in my mind. "I think …"

"Gemma." Alex put a hand under my chin, and the nick of his skin ripped me out of my daze. "Get us out of here."

This time I shut my eyes and pictured the first place that came to mind. We'd escaped there before. Viva Las Vegas. But something was stuck—blocking me from going. I opened my eyes and caught Laylen and Aislin swapping knowing smiles.

"They have praesidium on them," I whispered. "There's nothing I can do. Unless we run."

Alex's fighting face elevated to the challenge. He spun and within seconds, his body rammed into Laylen's. They collided to the frost-bitten ground, turning into an enormous snowball rolling around as they threw punches and cracked knuckles at each other. My gaze zipped to Aislin, who was watching me with cruelty in her eyes.

"Sucks doesn't it." She twirled her hair around her finger carelessly as she took lazy steps toward me. "Feeling so vulnerable, yet you can't do anything about it."

I got the feeling that this was much deeper than just the Mark of Malefiscus.

"I had to sit there and watch you bat your eyes at him like some kind of lovesick girl." Her high-heeled boots clicked against the ice. "Watch the way he looked at you until it almost drove me mad." She was right in front of me, our eyes locked, waiting for the right time to make the first move. "But those days are almost over. Soon you'll be gone—dead, rotting in the ground."

She's not herself. "Aislin, you don't have to do this. We're friends."

"Friends?" she whispered and then her hands ignited.

96

Without hesitation, I attack, slamming into her and sending us to the ground. Her hands burnt out when they hit the snow. I landed on top of her, not sure what to do. This was Aislin, mark or no mark, and I didn't want to hurt her. But then she got this look in her eyes, like she would do anything to hurt me. As her hand lifted, I smacked my knuckles hard into her cheek.

"Sorry," I apologized like an idiot.

She laughed, throwing her head at me and flipping us to the side. My head smacked into the ground, spots of snow stinging my eyes. I reached for her coat pocket, knowing that was where the praesidium had to be. But she bit my hand and I let out a painful cry. More garbage cans toppled over as Alex and Laylen rolled farther away.

My distraction allowed her to bite me again, cutting my skin this time. And that was it. I'd had enough. I clocked her again, this time not holding back. While she was recovering, I tore her pocket open, the purple marble of praesidium bouncing onto the ice. She grabbed my hand as I reached for it. I slid my legs over, nudging it with my shoe, and watched as it barreled for Laylen and Alex.

Then I shoved away from Aislin, trying to get to Alex, so I could take us away from here. But Aislin grasped my ankle, flinging me back down to the ground. I braced myself against the ice, turning over in time to see a ball of light moving for me.

I didn't think.

I just went.

Gemma 18
(Gemma)

Somehow I made it away, landing on the checker boarded living room floor. But I wasn't alone. A crazed Aislin was still gripping onto my leg, her eyes wide and murderous.

"I have to take you to him," she said, dazed and rabid. "I have to take you to him." Her nails dug into my arms.

"Adessa!" I screamed, praying the witch was home and wasn't inked with the mark.

By the scared look on Aislin's face, I was guessing she didn't. Aislin knew she was in trouble. But the house was as still as a statue and she relaxed, her fear replaced by delight.

"Guess she's not home." Aislin leapt to her feet. *"Duratus."*

I scurried to my feet, but the giant ball of light hurtled into my chest. At first, I thought she took my life like the last witch. But then my muscles went rigid and I lost all control of my body. I crumpled to the black and white tiled floor, my head clipping the corner of the apothecary table. My brain sung and my body throbbed.

Her fingers reached for my locket. "Guess it's not working anymore, or maybe I'm just too strong for sugilite." She snapped the chain from my neck, coiling it around her finger. "It's an immobilizing spell by the way." Her clarification was unnecessary since I couldn't move "Sucks doesn't it—not being the one in control."

She smacked her lips together. "I'm not sure what to do with you." She roamed around the room, running her fingers along the knickknacks on the shelf. She picked up a figurine of a woman with beautiful wings—a Black Angel. She turned it in her hand. "You know I'm supposed to take you to my father. The mark's begging me to. But I don't know. I'd like to see you suffer a little before I do that." She stared at the figurine with a spiteful look in her eyes I didn't like. "I'll be right back," she said, like she had just created the most evil plan in the world. "Don't go anywhere." Then she grinned and with a swish of her hands, vanished in a cloud of smoke.

That was a new trick too—apparently being evil made her more powerful.

All I could do was wait there helplessly until she came back.

Adessa had a dripping faucet somewhere in the house. It was driving me crazy as I lay on the floor, wondering what on earth Aislin was going to return with. Even though she was working with the dark side, part of me hoped it wouldn't be that bad. She was Aislin. But deep down, I knew it didn't matter. She had been brainwashed by the most evil man I knew—Stephan.

Finally, I heard a thump from inside the house. It was time to find out what Aislin was going to do to me.

But it wasn't Aislin who entered the room.

Adessa's golden cat-shaped eyes landed on me. "Gemma."

I tried to nod, but my head was a numb useless lump.

"Why are you …" She glanced around as if she sensed something was wrong. Then she swept her long black hair out of her face and knelt down beside me. She inspected me over and then she yelled, "*liberum.*"

I was instantly free and jumped to my feet, wanting to get as far away from this place as possible. "We have to get out of here."

"Why?" she asked. "Gemma, why are you here?"

I gave her a quick recap of all the stuff that had been happening.

"So Aislin has the mark, but she can remove the mark?" She ambled the room, her long navy dress flowing along the floor. "And you don't know where she went?"

I shook my head, urging her toward the doorway. "That's why we need to get out of here."

Adessa held up her hand. "We don't need to go any-where. We can fix this."

100

Suddenly, I feared she might be marked. My eyes took in her arms and neck, the places where it was most likely to be hidden. But her honey skin was mark free.

"Do you remember how she did it?" Adessa asked. "How Aislin removed the mark?"

"Kind of," I said. "I mean, yeah, I think so."

"Tell me and try to remember every little detail," she said, taking a seat on the purple velvet sofa.

"She could come back any minute," I warned. "We should go."

Adessa deliberated this and then stretched her hand, pointing to the ceiling. "*Me tenebris et tueri nos.*" A dark cloud rotated from her hand, casing the ceiling with a smoky sheet of black. "There." She dusted her hands off. "We have a few minutes. Now go ahead and try to explain it to me."

My eyes were wide as I took a seat. "The first thing she did was go to the graveyard to summon some kind of witch spirit to give her more power. Then she created the spell. First, she cuts into the middle of the mark so that blood drips out."

"To bleed out the evil." Adessa nodded, understanding. "Yes, that makes sense."

"Then she inserts some potion—I think she called it *Vitis vinifera*, which is supposed to free them from the evil connection," I said. "Then the last thing she does is chant some sort of spell ... *liberare vos ligaveris.*" God, I hoped that was right.

101

Adessa looked like it was making sense. She hopped to her feet, threw open the apothecary table, and it was filled with baggies of herbs. She took one out. "Does this look like the *Vitis vinifera* she used?"

The green crushed leaves did look familiar. "I think so. But it doesn't matter if you have all the stuff. You need the power of that ghost flame woman."

Adessa's eyes were kind. "Has Laylen ever told you anything about me?"

I wasn't sure how she wanted me to answer. "Um ... a little."

"Well, did he ever mention how old I was?"

I shook my head, not daring to utter an age, afraid if I said something older, she'd freak out like Sophia use to do. Thinking about my cold-hearted grandmother, sent a chill down my back. I hated thinking about the soulless years I spent with her. I remembered when Aislin finally broke down and told me Sophia and Marco were dead. She'd discovered this information when she'd been trying to lo-cate Keepers with a Tracker Spell, only the spell had informed her they no longer existed, which meant they had to be dead. The Tracker Spell didn't explain how they died though, but I knew that Stephan was probably behind it somehow. Just like he was behind most deaths.

Honestly, I had mixed feelings about their deaths. I was sad, but at the same time empty. I understood they'd been brainwashed during all those years of torture, yet the cold and harsh way they'd treated me was still a fresh wound. I'd spent much of my life being ignored by them as they'd let me sink into a lonely hole.

"I'm one-hundred and fifty-eight," Adessa replied and I blinked out of my trance. "And do you know how I lived this long without aging?" I shook my head and she rose to her feet. "Because I'm powerful."

I hated to break it to her, but if she was that powerful, she would have figured out her own spell. As if to prove me wrong, she flung her hands out to her side. Her head fell back, chin tipped to the smoky ceiling. "Isabella, come to me!" A fire burst through the air and the flaming woman materialized, letting out a deafening wail. I covered my ears as Adessa chanted magic under her breath, finally settling the fire woman down.

"You've been hiding something from me Isabella," Adessa warned. "Is there something you'd like to tell me?"

The fire woman hissed flames at Adessa's face.

"Don't take that attitude with me," Adessa said. "You've been lying to me for a very long time."

The flame woman tipped her head back and wailed.

"Stop sulking and hand it over." Adessa stuck out her hand and the fire woman let out a huff, blowing a breath of smoke and fire into Adessa's palm.

"Go now." Adessa flexed her hand. "And don't come back until you're sorry for what you did."

The flame woman dissipated and Adessa turned, smiling. I was pretty sure my jaw was hanging to the floor

"Now that that's taken care of." She shut the lid of the apothecary table. "I think I can make this work. But I'm going to need your help with something first—something that's very dangerous, but very important to me."

"Okay," I said, not surprised, because danger seemed to be my middle name. "Tell me what it is."

Chapter 19
(Alex)

I was going to kill him, strangle him until he died. At least I wanted to. But I wouldn't—or couldn't. Killing Laylen would nearly kill Gemma and she'd hate me for it. Besides, that'd be stooping to my father's level. No matter how hard he tried to turn me into one of his murderous soldiers, I refused to give in. I had to be stronger than he was. If anything, to save Gemma from dying.

So I held back on the strangling, instead knocking him in the side of the head with a snow shovel I stole off someone's back porch. Once he fell unconscious, I tucked his body under a tarp, beside a pile of firewood. Then I stood there in the darkness, trying to come up with some kind of plan that would salvage this mess. I had an unconscious, killer vampire in front of me and the two people who could take me away were missing.

There was only one thing to do. Go back to the Banshee and find out what happened. Then maybe I could figure out my next move.

She was wailing when I arrived, a cry of death, perhaps for me. I barged in, not bothering to knock and the pleased look on her face was enough that I saw red. I shoved her back and she tripped twisting her ankle as she fell to the floor.

"Who are you?" I demanded.

She smirked despite the pain. "Don't you think I should be asking you the same thing?"

"You don't get to ask the questions here." I squatted down beside her, pointing my knife at her throat. "Now who are you?"

Her eyes widened, the color shifting from green to blue and her hair from brown to blond.

"You're the Banshee from the alley," I said. "Why are you here?"

"You didn't think Draven would just hand you the information, did you? Who are you really? And why do you want the help of a Banshee?"

"He didn't just give it to me." My jaw tightened at the idea that this was just a set up—a very long, waste of time, set up. "I have to pay him back later."

"And you will," she said. "But we needed to see why you seek her. Why do you need a Banshee?"

"I'm not telling you anything, until you tell me why you brought me out here."

"Because this is the entrance to the Afterlife," she gestured at the blackened walls. "This is where you cross over."

"I'm not going anywhere." I had an idea. "Where's my mom? I know you know."

Her breath was venomous. "We don't just give away information about our kind."

My knife was at her. "Where is she? Tell me where she is!"

"In hiding." She sneered. "In a place where no one wants to hide."

I grabbed the Banshee by the collar of her shirt and yanked her toward me. "Where? Tell me."

"I will." She grinned slyly. "But it'll cost you."

Chapter 20
(Gemma)

"Tesha's a friend of mine," Adessa clarified, but I still wasn't thrilled about the idea. "If we can just get back to the house, I can take the mark off her."

"But what if it doesn't work." My eyes were fixed on the bright neon lights of the building. Standing in front of the glass doors, was a short woman with choppy hair, pointy ears, and turquoise eyes—Tesha. At first I thought she was a pixie or something, but I wasn't even sure if pixies existed.

Adessa explained that Tesha was a vampire friend of hers and that she'd somehow gotten branded with the Mark of Malefiscus. I tried to tell her a million times that it was a bad idea, because the last thing I wanted to do was take down a vampire when Aislin and Laylen were running around, doing who knows what. But when I saw the way Adessa looked at Tesha, I wondered if she might have been more than a friend.

"Alright, do you have a game plan?" I asked, peeking over the hood of the truck we were hiding behind.

Tesha was chatting with a man twice her size. I wasn't sure what breed he was, but the blue glow in his eyes made me guess he wasn't human.

"I was hoping you had one," Adessa said with a sigh. "I've been trying to get to her for weeks, but it's useless."

I frowned. I had a plan, but I wasn't very fond of it. "Okay, I'm going to foresee my way over there, grab her, and blink us back here—you better be ready to work the spell."

Adessa nodded, opening up the baggy. "I will, but be careful."

"Give me the knife." I shoved my hand at her.

Adessa shook her head, pulling the knife closer. "You can't hurt her."

"I'm not," I said. "But I'm not going in unarmed either."

Reluctantly, she handed over the gold-bladed knife. "Please, don't hurt her."

"I won't." *Unless I have to.*

"You'll have to be the one to puncture her mark." She tapped her left arm. "It's on her left wrist."

I put on my game face, even though I was scared out of my mind. "Be right back."

I shut my eyes and pictured the front door of the casino where Tesha stood. In a heartbeat, I had foreseen my way over, but managed to land myself between the tall man with glowing eyes and Tesha.

Their eyes darkened and the blue-eyed man reached for me.

"Sorry, not going to happen," I said and forced him back. He barely stumbled, but I grabbed Tesha's arm and whisked us away to Adessa.

As soon as we hit the asphalt, I shoved Tesha to the asphalt. Her fangs snapped out, sharp and long, and she nicked my arm. I snatched her wrist, fighting her as I made the incision on her left wrist where the triangle traced her skin. She snarled her fangs at me and then, as if she couldn't resist herself, bit into her own arm where blood was starting to pool.

"Adessa!" I shouted and Adessa knelt beside us, her hands trembling as she opened the bag of *Vitis vinifera*. She crumbled it into the open wound and it mixed with the blood. Again, Tesha nicked my skin with her fangs and I slapped her. She blinked, stunned, and Adessa looked like she was going to cry.

"Say the spell," I ordered. "Now!"

With a nod of her head, Adessa's lips parted. *"Liberare vos ligaveris!"*

Then we watched as the mark slithered away, off Tesha's arm and onto the ground, like a snake. Even though I had seen it before, it still got to me; the way the

110

mark kept going, toward the entrance of the casino, as if going to seek another.

I was on my feet before the next breath left my lungs and I stomped on the snake over and over again until it was smashed into the ground.

"Well," I said. "I think I just figure out how Aislin and Laylen were marked."

But Adessa wasn't listening as she seized Tesha in her arms.

"I'm so sorry." Tears poured down Tesha's cheeks.

"It's not your fault," Adessa said, smoothing Tesha's hair. "It's no one's fault."

Guilt choked at me, strangling away my oxygen. It was my fault.

Adessa helps Tesha to her feet.

"And who's this little warrior?" Tesha asked, wiping tears from her eyes.

Aislin gave her the quick details of who I was and what I could do. Although, there wasn't any mention of the star. But I'd be surprised if they didn't know. Word had spread that the girl with the violet eyes was *the one*..

We Foresaw back to Adessa's house, Tesha awing over my gift. We crowded around the couch, waiting for Aislin to make her grand entrance. The tick of the clock was driving me mad, along with everyone's restlessness.

"Where the heck did she go?" I muttered, tapping my foot against the floor, anxious to get this over with and make the lives of at least two people right again. "Maybe I should—"

But then she appeared like a ghost, only she wasn't a ghost. She was a very powerful witch that wanted to hurt me, her green eyes glowering with murder. And she wasn't alone.

"Remember these," Aislin sneered, jerking at the chains of a woman wearing a leather dress. Her black hair waved to the bottom of her back and her laced-up leather heeled boots clicked across the floor. The recognition in grey eyes told me she was the same Black Angel from the Black Dungeon.

She snapped out her wings, like a giant crow, ready to eat me alive. Aislin started to laugh hysterically, and I was beginning to wonder if an evil Aislin meant a crazy Aislin.

The Black Angel strolled toward me, her wings so wide they knocked things from the shelves, sending glass shattering to the floor.

"Take care of Aislin," I shouted to Tesha and Adessa. "I'll handle this." But my head laughed at me, because I had no clue how to kill one of these things. The only thing I knew about them was a) whoever freed them from their cage become one b) they were angels from hell and c) they liked to wear a lot of leather.

I tried not to look her directly in the eyes as I circled her. She turned, following me with her gaze, her lips snarling. I dared a glance at Aislin and was relieved to see Adessa was making the cut, while Tesha pinned Aislin down and covered her mouth. I kept moving, wanting to distract the Black Angel so Adessa could complete the spell and get the mark of Aislin.

But then she began to flap her wings and it was like a wind storm had blown through the room. I blinked and shielded my eyes from the flying glass and papers. The Black Angel growled and all my attention focused to her. It was like I was paralyzed, a helpless victim, as she sauntered toward me, grey eyes desperate to be free from the chains. My hands raised on their own, bounded by invisible strings the Angel controlled. I reached for the cuffs that trapped her wrists and made her a prisoner. And with the strength of a Keeper, I broke her free. The metal fell to the floor and the Black Angel shrieked with freedom. A loud boom reverberated through the house and the ceiling began to collapse.

I hit the floor, flat on my stomach, searching through the fallen debris. Finally, the air settled and I dusted myself off and got to my feet. I blinked at Aislin, Adessa, and Tesha, all their eyes filled with fear.

But I was glad for the fear in Aislin's eyes, because it meant she was back.

"What was that?" I asked, picking a piece of ceiling out of my hair.

"Gem-ma," Aislin stuttered, which was weird because Aislin never stuttered. Then she lifted her hand, pointing her finger to the side of me. Instinctively, I jumped, discovering an unknown woman close. She nipped her teeth and then grinned.

"See you in hell." She winked. Then with a puff of smoke, she was gone.

As the wheels clicked in my head, I glanced down at my arms. The first thing I saw was the same set of black symbols that traced Laylen's arm—the Mark of Immortality. Then I inched my hand behind me, touching the softness of the feathers.

"Oh my God." My hand dropped. "I have wings."

Chapter 21
(Alex)

It was going to cost me. A lot. More than my life. More than a year working for Draven. The damn Banshee wanted my soul and she'd led me out here thinking she could trick me into giving it to her. Apparently when someone sacrificed their own life, their soul was worth more. So if Gemma or I had drunk the poison she sent us to collect, our soul would belong to her and give her more power.

It was always about power

What the Banshee didn't realize was that my soul belonged to someone else. It was something Gemma still didn't understand—that no one understood. My soul belonged to her. And I wasn't speaking in an I love you kind of way. I'd actually given her some of my soul. When we'd made the forever blood promise, cutting our hands and uttering the forever words, it had been sealed by more than our blood. It had been sealed by our souls.

The night I'd wandered over to her house, the day when her emotions revived, I'd had a hunch that something might happen. I was still brainwashed by my father, but all that time away from her finally took me over. And I knew I had to see her. I made sure to keep my distance, staying in the shadows, watching her through her bedroom window. She seemed lost, like she didn't know what to do with herself, and my heart ached to go save her.

But my mind told me to leave.

As I'd started to go, I felt the strangest thing, like I was leaving my body, yet I still stayed on the ground. I clutched onto the fence, gripping it so tight it cut into my hands. I couldn't breathe. I couldn't move. And then I saw Gemma at the window, staring at me as my soul reconnected with hers.

It wasn't the electricity that had done it. It was my soul breathing back life into its other half. Which might be why we had to die together.

I ran home after that and never said a word to my father. He would have killed me if I did. But I heard about it. Sophia had kept this list and she would keep track of every time she performed the *Unus quisnam aufero animus*—soul detachment—on Gemma. I guess her soul had been a tough one and kept trying to revive itself. But the last and final time it was preformed was right after I showed up.

February 8th. The very day our souls rejoined.

My father came in raging, saying Sophia had tried to detach it again, but this time it was sticking. Then he

116

forced me, like a puppet, to go to school and poke my nose around and find out what I could. But I was warned not to get close to her.

The sucky thing was I didn't even put up a fight.

That's why I couldn't make the deal with the Banshee woman. But it didn't mean I was going to give up.

I rounded the corner of the house, heading back to check if Laylen had run off. I wasn't sure how I was going to get out of Iceland. I couldn't fly since I didn't have my passport. If all else failed, I would just have to track down a witch. I ducked behind the house and peeked underneath the tarp. He was still there, drooling all over himself.

"What am I supposed to do with you?" I said to myself. "I'd just leave you here, but I'm pretty sure Gemma would kill me."

"I can fix him."

I whirled, my knife out of my pocket before she could even work up a flinch. "Where is she?"

My sister threw her hands in the air. "She's fine. I'm fine." She rolled up her sleeves and the mark was no longer on her arm.

"So Gemma kicked your ass." I grinned.

She glared, but then shook her head. "We need to go."

I nodded my head at the wood pile. "You want to take care of him first."

"Oh, yeah." She seemed a little out of it, even for her, blinking confusedly. She rushed over to Laylen, giving a sad sigh as she worked her magic on him. Moments later, there was this strange snake thing moving toward me.

"Step on it!" she cried.

I stomped on it hard. "What was that thing?"

"That was the mark." She stood, dusting her hands. "And apparently, it doesn't die when it's removed."

I lifted the bottom of my shoe, pulling a face at the black goo. "So that's how you guys went craz … how you got the mark."

She scowled. "Yeah, from now on, they need to be stomped on."

Laylen woke up, confused and grabbing his head. "What happened? And why does it feel like someone punched me."

"No one punched you." I helped him to his feet. "I hit you in the head with a shovel."

He blinked, dazed, and I decided not to mention he'd bit Gemma because his own guilt would be more than enough.

"So where are we going?" I asked Aislin. "Back to the house?"

She glanced around nervously. "We're going to Adessa's."

"That's where you ended up?" I cocked an eyebrow. "Why?"

"It was Gemma," she replied, brushing the snow off Laylen's back. "And it's a good thing she did because it was Adessa who got the mark off me."

118

We huddled together, preparing to go to Vegas.

"But I have to warn you," she said. "You might want to prepare yourself."

I didn't have time to ask her why as she transported us away.

Chapter 22

(Gemma)

When I saw them, I took cover behind one of the purple velvet sofas.

"What the hell is that?" Alex asked in disgust and I wanted to cry, but at the same time kick him for being so judgmental.

"Gemma." Aislin's voice was gentle. "You can come out. I promise you're okay."

Yeah, easy for her to say. She wasn't the one with wings—very heavy wings—sprouting out of her back.

"I'd rather not," I called over the sofa, wishing I could curl up in a tiny ball.

"I don't understand," Laylen said. "What is that thing?"

Well, at least he was back to his old self.

"They can see your wings," Aislin called out. "They're sticking up behind the couch."

"Wings!"

"Wings?"

I sighed, rising to my feet. I felt like an animal in a zoo, their wide eyes on me, making me feel ashamed. It was bad enough I had wings coming out of my back, but somehow, I also ended up in the Black Angel's clothes. I had a dress on that barely covered the top part of my legs, and shoes which added more height to my already ridiculous tall frame. Laylen's blue eyes met mine, and I wanted to run up and give him a big hug because I could see he was himself again. But I didn't, fearing I'd freak him out.

I avoided Alex's eyes all together, because, let's face it, he was definitely prejudice when it came to things that weren't human.

"There was an accident," I said to the wall.

"What kind of accident?" Laylen asked, astonishment in his voice.

"I did it." Aislin started to cry. "It was my fault. I brought the Black Angel here."

I turned to her. "It's not your fault. You weren't yourself."

Tears flowed down her cheeks. "Yes it is."

"It's not your fault," I repeated. "If it wouldn't have been for me, the mark would have never gotten so out of control."

But she continued to sob and I felt him move toward me, my senses drawn sharply to him, even with the wings. He didn't say anything, only turned me to face him. I tuck my head down, mortified. But he put a finger under my

121

chin and elevated it up, so I had to meet his eyes, which were all over me, warming my skin with embarrassment.

"You'll be fine," he said with a relieved sigh "We still have time. We can still change you back."

"But I don't want anyone to have to take my place." I frowned.

"Don't worry," he said. "We're not going to do that. We'll find another way to get those wings off you. But we have to hurry, before you completely transform."

I let out a breath of relief. "I thought I was going to be stuck like this forever."

He shook his head. "But we have to hurry. You're still you right now, but you won't be for long if we don't move quickly." He paused, his eyes doing a quick sweep up my body, and a dark look crossed his face. "You can keep the dress, though, if you want to."

I stared at him blankly, but on the inside my heart was about to explode. "Keep looking at me like that," I said, my voice surprisingly steady. "And you're going to kill us both right where we stand."

He shrugged. "I'm just saying." He checked me over again and then turned to Aislin and Laylen. "So where's Adessa?" he asked. "We're going to need her help."

"She left," Aislin said. "With her ... friend. They said they were going into hiding until all this crap was over."

"Which will be soon," I said. "Alex and I found a way."

Alex shook his head. "Not yet. I still haven't found out where my mom is."

Aislin's eyes popped wide. "Our mom."

I elbowed Alex in the side. "You didn't tell her?"

He winced, clutching his side. "Ow … you're like freakishly strong now."

"And immortal." I stuck out my arm.

Alex snatched it, tugging me to him. He blinked at the Mark of Immortality, then let me go and headed for the front door.

"Wait. Where are you going?" I chased after him, wings slamming into the walls.

"To find a witch," he explained. "So we can get those things off you."

"Wait," Aislin said, racing after him. "I'm going with you."

Alex paused, looking at me. "Are you going to be okay?" His eyes wandered to Laylen. "By yourself."

I shooed him away. "Go, I'll be fine." But then I pulled him back, looking at the Mark of Immortality on my arm. "Are you sure we want to change it." I almost gagged on my words. "Because this could maybe help us—if I don't die, neither can you."

"It's not worth it," he said. "Besides, you wouldn't last long. You'd become one of them."

I leaned in, lowering my voice. "I thought you said I was supposed to get stuck in a cage."

He gave me a soft pat on the wings, ticking the black feathers. "Give it time and you will. You're in transition."

I glanced at Aislin. "How did you free her?"

Aislin's face twisted with confusion. "I used magic. A spell I didn't even realize I knew. It was weird, but I seemed to know a lot of spells I'd never heard of—darker spells." Then she sighed, reached in her pocket, and retrieved my locket. "Sorry I took it."

"It's okay." I put my locket back on and then gave Alex a heavy stare. "Are you absolutely sure you don't want to keep me like this."

He pressed back a smile. "I'm not going to let you turn into an Angel of Hell."

"Fine." I sighed. "I just wanted to make sure this wasn't our way out of dying."

"We'll find a way." He touched the feathers on my wings and this time I shivered. "I promised I'd save you and I will. Just not this way."

They left, slamming the door behind them and Laylen and I were left alone. An awkward silence built between us. Even worse, we both knew it wasn't because of my wings or the weird leather getup I was wearing.

"So," he began, staring at the black and white checkerboard floor. "How bad was I?"

"You don't remember?" I gasped.

"No, I remember, well at least enough to know that I …" he trailed off awkwardly. "I was just asking you … I mean, you were the one that was hurt."

I touched my neck. The bite marks were gone, but I swear I could still feel them. "It wasn't that bad."

It was like he'd relapsed or something, his bright blue eyes a deep sea of shame. "Don't sugarcoat it for me."

I sighed. "You know what, you're right. It was bad. You scared the crap out of me." I walked across the room, tucking the hideous wings against my back. I stopped in front of him, throwing my arms around his neck. "But we've all done things we're not proud of. And we just have to live with it and move on. Our mistakes don't define us, it's what we do afterward—how we grow—that makes us who we are."

Wow. I wasn't sure if I was saying that more for him or myself.

He was quiet for a while and I started to think my little speech bombed. But then he sighed and hugged me tight.

"When did you get to be so insightful?" he asked with a soft laugh.

I loved to hear his laugh, because it was such a rare occurrence. "I learned from the best."

We stood there in the silence, hugging each other, wings and all.

Chapter 23

(Alex)

I hated leaving her, but there was no way I was going to let her come with me. Her violet eyes drew enough attention and now she had wings.

"How did you know about this, but I didn't," Aislin fought to keep up with me as I shoved my way down the crowded streets of Vegas, neon lights flashing, casino machines ringing. People were dressed in impersonator costumes, handing out leaflets, ignoring the vampires feeding in the shadows.

"I know a lot of things you don't," I said.

"Yeah, but I'm a witch. You'd think I'd know that there was a spell to remove the wings of a Black Angel without sending them to hell. Are you sure it'll take two witches though?" She cast a glace around the street. "It'd probably be easier if I could just do it."

"No you need a witch for each wing ... So this is where all the vampires, fey, and witches migrate to?" I ob-

126

served, changing the subject, worried if she found out how I knew about this she'd be hurt. "I guess it makes sense, going where it's more crowded, where there are more humans."

She shook her head, pushing a crying woman out of the way. "You could be a little bit more sympathetic you know. You don't have to be such a jerk all the time."

"And you didn't have to hall a Black Angel to the house," I said. "But you did."

Tears started to slip out and I shook my head. Aislin had always been a crier.

"Sorry." I gave her a pat on the back. "That was me being a jerk again."

"It's okay." She wiped her eyes with the sleeve of her shirt. "You're just stressed."

"No, I'm not." I scanned the crowd for a witch that wasn't marked. "Because I'm going to fix this." Then I spotted one, not too far off, head down, black hair a veil across her face, trying to conceal her identity.

"We also have another problem." Aislin was still chattering. "Aleesa's still missing, and I think we should —"

I stopped and Aislin ran into me. I pointed through the crowd. "There we go. I'm guessing she's unmarked."

When we were younger, before my mom vanished, she used to teach me all this stuff that, at the time, I'd thought was a useless bunch of information. Things like how to kill a Death Walker or where the City of Crystal was. Or how to shift a Black Angel back to human form.

Sometimes I wondered if she knew all of this was going to happen. Or maybe she just knew my father was a dick who wanted to kill the entire world and would never teach me how to protect it.

Aislin seized my arm. "Maybe I should handle this."

"Hey," I said. "I can be charming when I want to, you know."

She frowned. "No, you just think you can."

"I don't think this is going to be easy no matter who goes over there," I told her. "It might be better just to knock her out."

Aislin narrowed her eyes and put her hands on her hips. "That wouldn't be very nice."

"I'm not trying to be nice," I said. "I'm trying to save Gemma."

"Alright, just give me a few seconds." Then she disappeared into the mob and marched up to the terrified witch. She said something and then the witch followed her back. "She'll help." She smiled, pleased, because she was right and I was wrong. She raised her eyebrows at me. "Should we get going?"

I motioned down the street. "Go ahead, lead the way."

The witches name was Emma and her quiet, frightened demeanor on the streets was very misleading. Once she got going she wouldn't shut up, yammering about who she was and where she came from. But she was helping us out, so I tried to keep my mouth shut and just put up with it.

When we arrived at the house, the lights were off, the air dead quiet, the front door dripping with water.

We went inside and I motioned for them to stop. "Wait here. Something seems off."

My knife was already out of my pocket, positioned in front of me as I crept up the front stairs and pushed the door open. I was greeted by air so cold, it could only mean one thing—the Death Walkers had been here. I sprinted into the living room, the table, chairs, and floor frozen over. And in the center of all of it, a Death Walker laid dead, its rotting flesh iced over by its own chill.

"Dammit." I ran my fingers through my hair, tugging hard, as Aislin and Emma came rushing in.

"What is this?" Emma asked, panicking, backing for the door. "You said I'd be safe. What is this?"

"Oh my god." Aislin's jaw dropped to the floor. "They had to—they had to make it out."

I pointed to the ground, at the dead Death Walker. "Yeah, but who killed that?"

Before Aislin and I could react, Emma screeched and dashed out the door.

"Should I go chase her down?" Aislin asked.

I nodded and she spun, sliding across the floor as she raced for the door and ran out into the darkness of the street.

I kicked the apothecary table across the floor and squatted down, examining the Death Walker. It had been stabbed by the one thing that could kill a Death Walker. The Sword of Immortality—I could see the cut where the tip of the knife hand entered the chest. But how? My father had it.

"Where are you?" I muttered to the air, like she could hear me. I stood up, inspecting the room for anything that would lead me to her. But everything was blanketed by ice, except for the front window, which was shattered. I walked over, sticking my head out. And there it was, like a secret message. A single purple flower, lying on the sidewalk, whispering: *come find me.*

Chapter 24
(Gemma)

"You know what, I think I kind of like the wings." Laylen smoothed his hand over the feathers as we sat on Adessa's velvet sofa, waiting for Alex to come back with his brilliant plan to save me.

"Don't be weird," I joked, pulling a face at the wings.

"I'm not being weird." He gave me a teasing smile and then his eyes widened in mocked shock. "What if you can fly?"

"I can't fly," I said, but then I knitted my eyebrows together, staring at the black feathers. "Can I?"

"You should try it," he encouraged.

I sighed back against the couch, the wings creating an uncomfortable lump behind my back. "This sucks. I should be trying to find a way to get into the Afterlife, and instead I'm stuck here."

"We'll get it all fixed," he assured me. "We always do."

I wasn't so sure, though. And the Iceland thing was a dead end, for God knows what reason — Alex hadn't gotten around to explaining that one yet.

"I know." I kicked my boots up on the table, hoping my words were true.

He leaned back, resting his arms behind his head. "I can't believe they bailed — Adessa and her friend."

"Why." I looked at him. "Wouldn't you run away if you could?"

"Maybe …" He twisted at his lip ring. "Do you think maybe in another life, if we'd been born human, without marks, without all of this, we could have lived normal lives?"

"Maybe." But even the idea of being normal seemed unreachable.

"Do you think you and I would have been friends?"

I laughed. "I think no matter what, you and I will always be friends."

"What about you and Alex? Do you think you two would have been together, if the star and the promise never existed?"

I traced the scar on my hand, thinking about where it came from, and what it meant. Then I shut my eyes, listening to my heart beat, whispering to its other half. "Yes," I said and my words surprised him and me both.

He acted kind of uncomfortable, putting his shoes on the table, and then moving to the floor again. "Maybe one day that world will exist."

Maybe. If I could find a way to save Alex and me, without letting Stephan win. But at the moment, it wasn't looking very promising.

Suddenly I leapt to my feet and bolted for the door, stepping into the blackness of the night. Confused, Laylen hurried after me, his boots thudding loudly against the floor.

"What are you doing?" he asked from the stairs.

Checking left and right, I spanned my wings out. "Seeing if I can fly. It might be my only chance."

I flapped the giant bundle of feathers, back and forth and back and forth until the air encircled me and lifted me off the ground. I didn't go very high because I didn't want to be spotted. But I hovered around for a while. When I planted my feet back on the ground Laylen was grinning from ear to ear.

"See, not so bad," he said.

I curled the wings against my back. "I guess not, but it doesn't mean I want to keep them."

We exchanged smiles, like two children hiding a secret. I plucked a violet flower out of a flower pot hanging by the front door. I spun it between my fingers, thinking of my childhood hideout.

I didn't know who heard the crackle first. But we dove together, below the window as the sound of ice slithered through the house, chilling even the dessert air.

We breathed heavily, listening to the voices and shrieks breaking the quiet.

"Where are they!" Stephan growled. "They were supposed to be here."

I dared a peek through the frosted window.

He stood beneath the light, scar as noticeable as ever. Death Walkers surrounded him as he cussed them out and swung the Sword of Immorality in the air. He looked panicked, unlike his usual eerily calm self. Maybe this was all finally getting to him. Maybe he was starting to doubt himself.

Then I spotted a girl cowered next to him, mute and numb, her dark curly hair and yellow-eyes branding her a faerie. Aleesa.

Stephan breathed ragged and wild. "You guys failed me."

"Oh crap," I muttered. "Aleesa's in there."

Suddenly, for no reason other than he was pissed off, Stephan stabbed a Death Walker in the chest. It let out a cry, yellow eyes glowing with fire before scorching out completely.

Laylen and I exchanged a look. "He's worried we're going to pull this off," he whispered.

"We're getting close." But then I frowned, remembering that my death was nearing. "Maybe we should help Aleesa."

The window exploded against our ears and jagged glass landing in my hair.

"Time to go," I said, grabbing Laylen's hand as Stephan and the Death Walkers swarmed from the door.

But when we turned, there were only more black-cloaked monsters wanting to devour us.

Stephan strode in front of me, his eyes as wicked as ever. "Well, well, well, what do we have here?" His eyes examined me, his gaze lingering on the wings. "Looks like you ran into some trouble."

I gritted my teeth, hands clenching into fists. Laylen shifted in front of me, but I scooted my hand over to hold him back.

Stephan stared up the street. "Interesting choice to hide, especially since you've hid here before." He paused, letting out an exhausted sigh. "I wish you'd just give up. It'd make my life easier. But I guess I can't be too upset with all of this." He gestured over his shoulder, toward the city, and what I saw on his forearm sent a shudder through my body.

The Mark of Immortality.

I shook my head. "No."

Stephan turned his arm over. "Beautiful, isn't it? It's amazing how good I'm getting at creating marks. Although, I might keep this one for myself. I mean, what's the point of having the power of Immortality if I'm going to share it with everyone."

"It's still not over," I said. "You want to know why?" I leaned in, my voice as steady as a rock, even though my insides were trembling like an earthquake. "Because Alex and I our going to kill you." Instantly I swung my fist into his face, startling him, and everyone else.

He clutched at his nose, buckling back. "Get her!"

Death Walkers inched in, eyes twinkling like crazed fireflies. But I flipped out my wings, taking out some of the Death Walkers in the process. I was about to take us away when I caught sight of Aleesa, stuck in the middle of the mess. I backed away, stretching my wings as far as they would go, and twirled. A group of Death Walkers dropped to the ground like dominoes. I snatched Aleesa's hand and held on tight, even when she tried to jerk away. Then I encircled the three of us in a halo of feathers and let the crushed violet flower fall from my hand, hoping he'd figure it out. Ice frosted the tips of my wings as I took a deep breath and blinked us away.

Chapter 25

(Gemma)

"I think my wing's broken," I complained, tucking it close to my arm. "I think the Death Walker's ice did it."

From the safety of my old childhood hide out, Laylen inspected my wing, while Aleesa lay on the floor, unconscious. It was the only thing we could think of to keep her out of trouble until Aislin showed up.

"Does it hurt when I do this?" He softly brushed his fingers along the feathers.

"Ye-ah." I winced.

Laylen sighed and rested back against the dirt wall. "I'm not sure, it might be broken. Let's just hope Aislin and Alex show up soon. Although, I still don't get why you think they'll be able to find us."

I shrugged, leaning back against the wall. We'd pulled out a candle from the trunk and lit it, so we weren't smothered by darkness, but the shadows dancing in the light of the flame made me edgy.

"I just have a feeling." I didn't want to say the real reason, because I wasn't sure Alex would catch on. But the violet flower I hoped would be a good enough message — that he would think of the violet bush that conceal our childhood hideout and know where to look.

"What are we going to do?" I asked, running my finger down my Mark of Immortality. "He's Immortal now — not even Alex and I can kill him. Poor Aleesa."

Our eyes moved to where she lay, breathing heavy, her dark hair a tangled mess.

"I think we might have to find a safe place for her, after Aislin removes the mark." He rubbed his skin where his Mark of Malefiscus used to be. "She's almost like a child, you know. And things are getting too dangerous for her to be around."

I nodded. "But where? I mean, who can we trust?"

"I'm not sure. But I'd like to point out that Alex and you are never going to die, anyway. We're going to find another way to end this — and we'll find a way to remove the Mark of Immortality. I mean, we found a way to remove the Mark of Malefiscus, didn't we?"

"Maybe. Somehow." But I didn't completely agree with him. I wasn't sure we'd ever find another way because Alex and I dying was the original mapping of the world's future. Altering it again was out of the question.

"Nice punch, by the way," Laylen remarked with a proud smile. "I've been waiting for someone to do that to him for a long time."

I stretched my hand. "It did feel kind of good."

We smiled, but they were heavy smiles, burdened with death, life, and a responsibility no one should have to endure.

As more time drifted by, I started to worry that my little message to Alex was a dud. But then a puff of smoke clouded the tiny room, and two forms. Alex and Aislin appeared, blinking in disbelief. There wasn't a candle or amethyst in Aislin's hand, so she must have used her new little trick she learned during her brief trip over to the dark side.

My skin hummed elatedly as I jumped to my feet, but a sudden thought brought me to a halt. "Wait. Where's the witch?"

"Yeah ..." Alex shifted uncomfortably. "We kind of ran into a problem."

"What kind of a problem?" I itched at my wings. "You couldn't find a witch?"

Aislin raised her hand and a giant red X crossed the top of it. "This kind of a problem."

"What is that?" I swapped a worried glance with Laylen and he rose to his feet, brushing the dirt off the back of his jeans.

Alex sighed. "She's been branded."

Chapter 26

(Alex)

Aislin was taking forever and I grew tired of waiting for her to return with the witch, Emma. I stuffed the flower into my pocket and started down the street. I wasn't planning on going very far, wanting to remain close to the house in case she returned. But at the corner of the street, I noticed something odd. The Vegas lights had shut down, and smothered the city in blackness. The lamp posts on the roads were still lit, so there was a little light, but not much.

I had this irking feeling that this might have something to do with my sister, so I hurried across the street, continuing toward the dead city. When I reached the outskirts of the main road, I knew something was going down. The mutters and chants streaming through the night had a deeper meaning than I could understand. I moved up to the side of a large steel building, pressing my back against the wall, and trying to decipher what was going on. The voices spoke Latin, murmuring words of change and entrapment. Dammit, Aislin. What did you do?

I popped my neck and cracked my knuckles, preparing myself for a fight. Then I steadily stepped out into the street. Through the throng, Aislin stood on top of a stairway that rose to a towering building. An illuminating light tied her wrists and her eyes were wide beneath the low emergency lights.

Okay, so this was a mess. I was guessing that the rope was some kind of entrapment spell. I did a quick assessment of the crowd and noticed the abundance of star and crescent moon marks. So they were witches. But what did Aislin do to piss them all off?

Then one particular witch emerged, walking up to the top of the stairs. It was a witch who thought I was dead and knew Aislin could remove the Mark of Malefiscus.

Amelia.

So she'd tracked Aislin down on her own. But why the mobbing crowd?

"Welcome witches." She raised her hands in the air. "I've gathered you here today because I've discovered something I want to share with you all!"

The crowd of witches clapped and shouted their hoorays and I rolled my eyes at the ridiculousness.

"Thank you. Thank you." Amelia bowed her head like she was the Queen of the Sin City or something. Then she turned to Aislin. "This one right here has the power to remove the mark that threatens us all, that forces us to kill, forces us to spread our magic in the foulest ways." She gave a dramatic pause. "Yet, she does nothing to help us. She doesn't share her power or come to our aid."

"I have other problems to deal with," Aislin snapped, trying to free her hands.

But Amelia talked over her. "So let us strip her of her magic and forever brand her an enemy of the witch world."

Crap. It was time for a plan. With my head tucked down, I pushed through the crowd, moving slow to draw less attention. They all were chanting, low voices mixing with the wind. I reached the front line as Amelia lifted her hand toward the dark sky. I took off up the stairs, startling her. Aislin grinned and jumped to the side, slamming Amelia to the ground.

The crowd charged up the stairs roaring.

"What do I do?" I asked, reaching for the glowing rope, but then pausing. "How do I get it off?"

Aislin shook her head. "Just run!"

We sprinted up the stairs, toward the domed entrance of the building, a crowd of angry witches throwing magic at our heels. We ducked and weaved, trying to stay out of the way of flying flames, but one nicked Aislin in the hand. The light of rope burst into flames and she was freed. She touched my arm and suddenly we were back at Adessa's house, lying flat on our stomachs, on the icy floor.

"So where do you think they went?" She pushed to her feet, scratching at the back of her hand.

I removed the flower from my pocket. "I think she took them to our old hideout."

"The one in the forest?" She pulled a face at the lifeless Death Walker.

I nodded and put the flower away. "So can you take us there?"

She grinned, smoothing down her hair. "Of course." Then she extended her hand, but quickly pulled back. Across the top of her hand was a giant red X.

"Do I even want to know what that is?" I sighed. If it wasn't one thing, it was another.

She rubbed at the X. "I've been branded. No other witch will ever work with me again." She started to tear up.

"Relax," I said. "At least you can still do magic."

"Yeah, but no witch will ever work with me." She frowned. "Which means I can't perform the spell on Gemma."

"And no witches will break this rule?" I asked. "I mean it's just a mark."

"Just a mark," she said and I got her point. "This spell forbids witch magic to mix with my own, so it's not because they don't want to help me. It's because they actually can't."

"Why would they do that to you?" I asked, nudging the dead Death Walker away with my foot. "I mean, what was the point?"

"There was no point," she said. "Those spells they were throwing were all random."

"Alright, well I guess we'll have to figure it out another way," I said. "Know any witches you really trust?"

"The only one I trust went into hiding," she said. "And it's hard to find a witch that doesn't want to be found. Especially one as old as Adessa."

My mental stability was cracking. I tightened my hand, ready to punch a hole in the wall.

"Alex. I can try it myself. You're not giving my witch power any credit."

I shook my head. My mom had been very specific with her instructions on removing the wings of a Black Angel. Two lines of Wicca blood. "We'll figure something out. But right now we need to get out of here. I need to know if she's okay."

Aislin nodded. "Let's go to them."

***

The look on her face, when I told her the heart-crushing news was enough to kill me.

"So I'm stuck like this?" She frowned, her violet eyes forcing back the tears as she hugged her legs. "I'm stuck a Black Angel forever? What happens when I start changing? Am I actually going to turn into one of them?"

"We'll find a way," I told her. "I'm not going to let anything happen to you. I promise."

She nodded, tucking her wings in, one of them bent and crooked.

"What happened?" I touched the wing and she flinched in pain.

"The Death Walkers' ice did it," she said.

I arched my eyebrow. "So do you want to explain what happened with that? And why there's a dead Death Walker lying in Adessa's living room."

She sighed and told me a story with the most terrible ending I'd ever heard … so far.

"I can fix it. I can remove the Mark of Immortality." Aislin announced, before anyone could utter a word. "And I can fix her wings. I just need some time."

"We don't have time," I said. "In fact, we ran out of time quite a while ago."

"No, we haven't." She sucked in a deep breath. "This is what we're going to do."

Chapter 27
(Gemma)

"Black magic," Alex repeated not impressed. "That's your brilliant plan?"

"It's better than your plan," Aislin replied, annoyed. "Which is nothing."

Her plan was pretty simple on the surface. She wanted us to go to a Black Magic store so she could collect some items that would allow her to create a spell that would steal another witch's power. Then she'd have the power of two witches and could free me from the entrapment of the black-feathered wings.

The Mark of Immortality was going to be a little bit trickier. The first big problem was the shield spell on Stephan, but Aislin assured us, she had almost perfected the spell for its removal. For the mark, she would just tweak the spell she had been using to remove the Mark of Malefiscus. Big problem, though. That meant getting close to Stephan. When I pointed this out, she said one step at a time, which meant she didn't have an answer.

"Black Magic's dangerous," Alex warned. "You've told me that a thousand times."

"Life's dangerous." She gestured at me, at Laylen, then at Alex. "I mean, look at us. We're neck deep in danger all the time. It's who we are and I think it's time we start embracing it."

Personally I liked her speech, but Alex rolled his eyes. "So what? We just enter the Black Magic store and order these witches, who are evil, to give us the stuff so you can take away the power of another witch. Because I'm thinking witches might not be so excited about that." He pointed at her hand. "Or that."

"I'll wear gloves," she said, covering the X. "And I'll take Gemma with me."

I pointed at myself, not wanting to go anywhere looking like this. "Why me?"

"An Angel from hell." She grinned. "They'll eat you up."

Was that a good thing?

"So what? You two want to wander off to a witch store alone?" He let out a sharp laugh. "Because last time you two decided to do that, things didn't work out too well for you."

"We made it out," she argued, straightening up her shoulders. "And yeah, that's what we're doing. And you two can go find mom."

"So we can just fix everything at once," I said. "Sounds good to me."

Obviously, Alex wasn't on board with this. "You know, the last time I checked, you two weren't in charge."

"And neither were you," I said. He gave me a look that was mixed with frustration and a little bit of desire. "I think we should vote."

He folded his arms. "No way. I already know where everyone's vote lies." He glanced at Laylen, sitting by the dirt wall.

"Sorry, but I'm with them on this one," Laylen said, flicking a lighter on and off.

Alex shook his head, but then let out a huff. "Fine." He punched the wall to make a point that he was angry. "But hurry. You're going to start fading away and turn into a snarling Hell Angel."

"Meet you back here, then?" I asked, getting to my feet, the flame of the candle flickering with the sway of my wings.

"Hold on," Laylen said. "You guys are forgetting something."

We stared at him uncomprehendingly.

"Aleesa." He nodded his head at her.

She was still lying on the floor, drooling away, and I hoped I hadn't done any permanent damage to her when I'd knocked her out.

Aislin sighed. "I think it might be time to take her to the faerie realm."

"But I thought she was a forbidden breed," I said. "Wouldn't they like hurt her or something?"

"They won't hurt her," Aislin said. "But they won't be too welcoming either. It's probably the safest place for her though, at least for the time being."

"Is it safe?" I asked. "Because the faeries here are marked."

"I've heard that some of the faeries have gone into hiding there." Alex stuffed his hands in his pockets and kicked at the dirt. "So I'm sure it's safe."

"There's only one way to find out." Before anyone could take their next breath, Aislin vanished with Aleesa.

"She's letting this power thing get to her head," Alex muttered.

"I'm sure she'll be fine." I sat down on the ground by Laylen, crossing my legs.

Alex let out a snort as he dropped down on the floor. "The last time she ran off by herself, she was chased down by a mob of witches."

"She'll be fine," Laylen assured him. Or maybe he was assuring himself. He flicked his lighter open, burning a string hanging from his black jeans.

"So what happened back in Iceland?" I asked Alex, inching away from him and the fiery static. "Did you figure out if the Banshee was your mother?"

Laylen pulled a face. "What the heck were you two doing in Iceland, with a Banshee?"

I slumped against the wall, poking each of them with the tip of a wing. "Trying to save the world."

"The Banshee was a dead end," Alex said, digging into the dirt with his knife. "We're going to have to find another way to find my mom."

We all sighed simultaneously and the candle flickered.

"What a bummer." Laylen frowned, scratching at his Mark of Immortality. Then suddenly his eyes lit up. "If Aislin can remove Stephan's mark …"

"You want her to remove yours?" I touched the symbols on his forearm. "You want to be mortal?"

"I want to be normal." He winced. "And that might be as close as I can get."

When Aislin returned, we all jumped at her sudden appearance. Her hair was like a wild jungle animal, her breath heavy, her eyes wide.

"Faeries are mean," she breathed, fixing her hair. "Like really, really mean."

"You didn't know that?" Alex and I said at the same time.

"What happened?" Alex asked. "Did they take Aleesa in?"

Aislin stared at the vacant spot beside her. "Does it look like she's here?"

Alex glared. "Obviously, but there wasn't any problems?"

"Oh, there are problems." She picked a leaf out of her hair and flicked it to the floor. "I now owe Luna a magic spell that will free her to this world."

"Who's Luna?" I held up my hands. "Wait. Let me guess. She's queen of the faerie realm."

"Empress," Aislin said like it meant something different. She erased a smudge of dirt off her cheek. "And she's not very nice either."

"So what?" Alex's face heated with anger. "You're just supposed to free her. That sounds like a stupid idea."

She shrugged. "It was the only way they'd let Aleesa stay there unharmed."

"You should have brought her back here then," Alex said.

"It was too late," she replied. "Once I was there, there was no turning back. Look, let's worry about that later. She's safe and I'll figure out a way around it after we fix the *bigger* problems." Her eyes landed on my wings.

"Is it just me," Laylen said, patting my shoulder. "Or does disaster seem to be drawn to us."

"It's not just you." I sighed. "But Aislin's right. We have other things to fix first."

Alex rubbed his temples tensely. "Alright, let's go then. I want to get this taken care of."

"So where are we meeting?" I moved to the other side of the small hideout. "Back here?"

151

He shook his head. "No, at your house. There's something I need from there anyway." Then he stuck out his hand. "Can I borrow your ring?"

I glanced at the purple-gemmed ring. "Why do you need it?"

"I promise I'll give it back," he said, insistent.

Reluctantly, I took the ring off and laid it in the palm of his hand. He closed his fingers around it and then we said our good-byes and headed our separate ways, hoping when we saw each other again we'd have fewer problems instead of more.

After Aislin dropped Laylen and Alex off at my house, we transported over to a Black Magic store called The Evil Side, which I thought was a lovely name. It looked just like one would imagine an evil magic. The windows were tinted with grime and the door had a sinister looking serpent on it. The roof shingles were rotting, the wood paneling peeling away.

"Ready for this?" Aislin asked, starting across the parking lot.

I pulled her back, my gaze glued to the store. "I think we should have a game plan, just in case."

"We already have one—you. Black Magic witches worship you. You're like their God … or Goddess."

"Still, I'd feel better … I mean, I can already sense the praesidium inside."

"Okay." She swept her hair out of her face. "We'll make sure to stay by each other at all times and if all else fails I'll transport us out of there." She grinned. "Because I can now do that, no assistance need."

I nodded warily and doing what I was supposed to, I stayed close to her as we headed across the parking lot and into the store. A bell dinged as we entered, the door swinging shut behind us. The air stunk of burnt herbs, smoke, and something else I couldn't place—and wasn't sure I wanted to place. The items littering the room made me want to stay in the dark with the inner workings of the Black Magic World. There were rows and rows of jars, filled with yellow liquid and parts that looked like they belonged buried. The statues on the shelves were twisted and torturous and the walls were black, the floor a blood red.

"Can I help you?" A tall witch, with golden eyes and hair as pale as snow, appeared in front of us. She looked us over, taking in my wings, then bowed her head. "We're so honored to have a Black Angel in our store. How can I assist you?"

Aislin shoved a list at her. "We need everything on this."

The witch ignored her, fascinated with me. "Is that why you've come—to collect the items from this list?"

"Yeah," I said self-consciously. "Can you help us?"

She nodded, excited I spoke to her. She snatched the list and scurried off to gather the items. Another witch entered from the back doorway, her hair as orange as fire. They exchanged whispers and then the orange-haired one greeted me.

"It's a pleasure to have you in my store." She curtsied. "I'm Catalina and if you need anything at all, just let me know."

"Okay." I said and then she frowned, her eyes snapping cold.

"She hasn't even transitioned yet." Then she stormed for the other witch. "That's not a Black Angel, but a mere human with wings."

If only she knew how wrong she was. Still, the pale-haired witch scampered around, collecting the items on the list. Aislin and I roamed the store, not daring to touch anything, but needing to do something else besides stand there. I stumbled across a candle, perched on a shelf, blanketed in a layer of dust. There was a rainbow of colors wrapping around the wax and up the wick. It appeared to be glowing.

"What is it?" Aislin reached for it, but I smacked her hand.

"Don't touch it if you don't know what it is," I said, but couldn't seem to take my eyes off the magnificent looking candle either. It was hypnotizing.

"It's the Power of Entrapment candle." The paled-haired witch appeared over my shoulder. She picked up the colorful candle. "It traps the power of a witch inside their own body, at least while the wick burns."

"What about other kinds of power?" My hands trembled as I touched the candle. "Does it trap them too? Or is it just for witches."

She shrugged. "I guess it might, but what other power are you talking about?"

I shrugged and then Aislin and I traded looks, thinking the same thing.

"How much is it?" Aislin asked, reaching to unzip her purse.

"Oh, it's only for trade," she replied. "Catalina only makes trades for things as powerful as this, and it has to be a good trade."

"And I'm positive you two have nothing I want," Catalina barked from behind the glass counter.

The paled-haired witch sighed. "Sorry, she lacks people skills."

Frustration burst through me like an erupting volcano. "Are you sure there isn't anything at all we could trade for it?"

She eyed us over and I realized neither of us had anything, really. Aislin had her gloves and earrings and I had my necklace.

"Oh, that's pretty." Her fingers inched for the locket my mother gave me to protect me from magical harm.

I stepped back, shaking my head and my wings bumped the shelf. "Not that. Anything but that."

"Catalina, come look at this," she called out, eyes locked on my locket. "This one's got sugilite on her."

Catalina was over in a snap of a finger, grabbing my necklace without asking. "And it's wrapped by silver." She glanced at the candle and then at me. "You want the candle, give me the necklace."

"It's just a necklace." I clutched onto it for dear life, tugging it from her grasp.

"A necklace filled with sugilite! It's a very sought after stone in the Wicca world. After all, who doesn't want protection?"

I stared at my necklace, at the candle, and then at Catalina. The look on her face made me think this was no longer my decision. I unclamp the locket and handed it over to her greedy little witch fingers. The paled-haired witch tossed the candle at me and I hugged it to my chest, hoping it'd be worth it.

Chapter 28
(Alex)

I wasn't sure if the ring would work on me or not. But I had to try because I needed to talk to him. He knew things. I knew he did. His faerie blood connected with every breed of faerie in the world, including a Banshee. Honestly, I wished I'd started with him, and then it would have saved the bargain with Draven and the waste of a trip to Iceland. But what was done was done and there was no use dwelling on the past. I had to focus on the future.

Laylen was giving off a nervous vibe as we stood in Gemma's bedroom, where I knew the dead faerie would be, waiting for her to return.

"So what are we doing here?" Laylen looked around at the tan walls, tapping his fingers on his leg.

"We're looking for Nicholas," I showed him the ring.

"Why?" Laylen asked, sitting down in the compute chair. "Because he seems like the last person you'd ask for help."

"He's got faerie blood in him." I shoved the ring on my pinky, ignoring the fact that it was purple and obviously made for a girl. "He has to know something."

"See anything yet?" Laylen asked after a minute of silence.

I shook my head and let out an exasperated breath. "I figured it'd only work on her, but I had to try." I moved to take the ring off, but then I heard a voice and I paused.

"Look at you," Nicholas's voice swept through the room. "Trying to hunt me down for once?"

"Where are you?" I asked, knowing I had to keep my cool. At least for now.

"I'm dead," he replied. "So obviously, I'm a ghost, which means I'm anywhere I want to be."

I clutched my hands so tight the ring dug into my skin. "Where is she?"

"Who?" Nicholas asked. "The list of people you two are looking for is endless. I mean, there's Jocelyn and Alana and me."

The way he said Jocelyn's name made me question if he'd done something to her. The last time Gemma saw her she was a ghost and had disappeared with Nicholas. Then only Nicholas returned, saying Jocelyn was detained.

"Where is Jocelyn?" I asked, impulsively pulling out my knife.

Laylen rose to his feet and accidently knocked a CD on the floor. "Can you see him? He's not by me, is he?"

I held up a finger. "Not yet ...but ..."

158

"And you never will," he said. "I have nothing to say to *you*. Now go away and don't come back unless Gemma's with you."

"I'll tell you what. Show yourself and I'll make a bargain with you." I enticed, walking a thin line, because faeries were known for their tricks. And Nicholas was full of them.

"What kind of a bargain?" He bit the bait.

"The kind where you can live again."

Laylen shot me a baffled look and I nodded my head as a warning.

Nicholas was quiet, but this time I could hear him breathing, considering my offer. Then soundlessly he surfaced by the paneled window, next to an oblivious Laylen.

His eyes narrowed on me. "This better be good."

"Oh it is, but I want your info first." I flipped the knife in my hand, letting him know I had it. "Starting with the location of Jocelyn."

"You know that can't hurt me," he said, eyeing my knife. "I'm a ghost."

"Well, if that's true then I guess you have nothing to worry about." I stopped tormenting him with my knife and placed it on the dresser. "Now answer the question."

"First I need to know how you're going to save me," he said quietly.

I shook my head slowly. "You first."

We stared each other down, a challenge between the dead and the living. I remembered the days when I used to

159

beat the crap out of him to get him to talk. I missed those days.

"Fine, Jocelyn is gone," he said. "But I'd like to point out that I warned her they didn't like me down in the Afterlife because I'm only a half-breed."

"So she's stuck there because of you." I wanted to rip his head off. "And what do you mean gone?"

He shrugged and leaned against the wall. "Her essence crossed over. But it wasn't even supposed to be here to begin with. When we showed up in the Afterlife, Annabella collected her essence so she could cross over. So she moved on, past the ghost life."

"She's gone?" A lump formed in my throat. "Gemma won't ever see her again?"

"She was never supposed to be here," he repeated. "She had a brief gap between her death and her body, where she could roam free, but unlike me it was her time to go."

"And what about my mom?" I wondered. "Do you know where she is?"

A deceitful look crept across his face. "Isn't she dead too?"

"Watch it," I warned. "It's your life at stake here. Not mine."

"Oh, I beg to differ." He laughed and I lunged for him, but only grabbed air. It threw me off balance and I smacked my head on the wall.

160

"What are you doing man?" Laylen gaped at me like I'd lost my mind.

"Trying to kill a ghost," I growled, spinning in circles.

Nicholas laughed again. "This is so much fun. It really is, seeing you like this."

That was it. Time to move. "Let's go." I stormed for the door, hoping Nicholas would bite the bait again.

"Wait," he called out.

I smiled to myself as I turned. "Yeah."

"I might know where she is," he said, standing closer than I anticipated. "Although, I thought you'd have figure it out on your own, since you've been trapped there yourself before."

"What are you ..." And then it clicked. "Are you saying that she's in the City of Crystal, trapped against the massive crystal?"

He grinned and I had my answer.

"Take me there," I demanded and picked up my knife.

"Not until you tell me how I can become undead."

"When we free the Lost Souls," I said. "I'll make sure to include your name."

"You say it like you're the one going." He snickered. "That'll never happen."

I gestured around the room. "She's not here is she?"

He laughed, hunching over, gasping for air. "You still don't get it. It has to be her—it always has and always will."

Laylen walked out the door, his hands cupping his head. "This one-sided conversation is too much. I can't take it anymore."

I turned my attention back to Nicholas. "Not if I do it without her knowing about it."

"You're still not getting it," he said, shaking his head. "You can't just change how it's supposed to be. That's what you mere humans don't get. Us Foreseers understand everything happens for a reason, even mistakes as great as Gemma's father, Julian Lucas committed. We are who we are. There's no changing it. It has to be Gemma. She was the one born with the Foreseer gift, the one destined to change the vision. And she's the one who has to make the bargain with Helena because she's responsible for the Lost Souls."

"But she didn't do it on purpose," I said. "She was only fixing her father's mistakes."

He shrugged half-heartedly. "Like I said, that was what she was destined to do, since the day she was born."

"And what about my mother," I snapped. "What does she have to do with this?"

"You can ask her yourself." He pulled out a red-ruby crystal ball and held it up between his fingers. "In the City of Crystal."

"What's wrong?" Laylen peeked his head back inside. "Is he being his usual annoying self, or did he finally hand the info over."

I ignored Laylen. "This is such crap."

162

"We all have to endure difficulty in our life," he said "Some just more than others."

Chapter 29

(Gemma)

"Stop picking at your feathers," Aislin said, mixing a bowl of green goo and leaves. "We don't know if it'll do anything permanent to you."

"But they itch like crazy," I whined, still scratching, feathers falling out and floating to my bedroom floor.

After we'd finished up at the The Evil Side, we'd transported to my house. But Laylen and Alex weren't there, so Aislin had jumped straight into witch mode, mixing her potion, while I sat on the floor itching at the feathers and staring at the rainbow candle, wondering what would happen if it worked. What kind of emotions would I feel? New ones?

I touched the back of my neck, thinking about the prickle and how I hadn't felt it in a while. Maybe because I'd felt everything. But that wasn't true. There was one thing I still didn't understand completely.

Love.

"It's like you're molting," Aislin observed with a smash of the spoon.

I glowered at her. "I'm not a bird."

"I know," she said "But you do have wings."

I plucked another feather and flicked it to the floor. "How long is that going to take?"

Another crush. "Not too much longer, but I still have to steal a witch's power."

I motioned at the boarded window. "Well, there's a ton out there. Take your pick."

"We can't find one there. When I take their power, whoever they are, they're going to try to kill me."

"But they won't have their power," I pointed out. "So you could just run."

She sighed, exhausted. "It'd be better if I just took it from someone far away from here, so they can't track me down."

"Have any place in mind?"

"Yeah ..." she trailed off, staring at the red X on her hand.

"Is this some kind of revenge plot or something?" I wondered, rubbing the dust off the candle. "Are you going back to Vegas to steal Amelia's power?"

"Who's Amelia?" She swished the bowl around.

I plugged my nose at the smell of her potion that reeked like rotten eggs and public bathrooms. "She's the witch who put that X on you."

"Good to know." She got this wicked look on her face.

165

I pointed a finger at her, rising to my feet and kicking up feathers. "This is a revenge thing."

"She branded me from the witch world," she said, her voice piercing with a grudge. "She deserves it."

"Okay, have your revenge." I waved my hand at her. "Am I coming with you?"

Her green eyes moved to my wings. "You draw a lot of attention."

"Fine." Usually I was an arguer, but it was better if I stayed behind, "I'll stay and build my nest."

She laughed. I laughed. And we had this weird, normal moment.

After she brewed her potion, she rinsed out the bowl in the kitchen sink and was on her way.

"If you're not back in a half-an-hour," I said, pointing at the wall clock. "I'm coming to look for you."

She thought this was funny for some reason. "I'll be back sooner than that."

Then she poofed away and it was just me and my empty house. For some reason I felt like I was back to square one, that I drifted back through time, to the old Gemma life. Only I had wings and was wearing a stupid leather dress and high-heeled boots.

I got up, deciding to scrounge through Marco and Sophia's room, for no reason other than I was bored. I flipped open the trunk and took out the photo's Sophia kept, wishing that I belonged in them—even just one. But every pho-to had the same similarity—none of them included me.

I pried out the bottom board and looked at my birth certificate. I thought of my father, trapped in his own mind, perhaps with the Death Walkers. Then my mother snuck into my thoughts; a life spent in The Underworld—something she did to herself. And now she was dead. Another thing done by her own hand.

"Mom," I called out to the empty room, but only my heart answered me. I tore the certificate up into tiny pieces and watched them float to the carpet. If I survived this, I would no longer be that girl. If I survived this, I would finally start my life.

I curled up in a ball, domed my wings around me, and cried in the silence of my own shell.

Chapter 30
(Alex)

It felt like I took a giant step backward. I was back in the City of Crystal and honestly, I was hoping I would never have to come back here again. Being strapped to that enormous fire ball was more painful than getting stabbed in the arm with a knife.

I had never been a fan of the City of Crystal. The crystal walls and ceiling made it feel like I was trapped in an ice cave. Then, of course there was Dyvinius. He creeped me out. I mean, the guy knew everything; what would happen with our lives, when we would die.

I suddenly had this urge to make a right instead of a left and head over the bridge, through the silver doors, to Dyvinius and demand to know if we made it—if Gemma and I would live. But instead I made a left, followed Nicholas up the crystal path, and to the door that sealed the crystal ball.

"So we're back here again," Laylen commented as Nicholas opened the door. "I was actually hoping we'd never have to come back."

"Me too, man." I stepped inside, glancing around, trying to disregard the energy flowing from the ball. "Why's she even here?"

"Who?" Nicholas asked. "Oh, you mean your mother."

I rolled my eyes. "Who else would I be talking about?"

Nicholas strolled up to the crystal and stared at the bodies, lifeless, chained, barely even human. "It really is a fascinating thing," he observed. "Drain the life of humans, to feed the crystal."

"It's a pointless sacrifice," I said, blinded by the blue glow. "No one needs to see what happens in the future. If it hadn't been for a Foreseer, we wouldn't even be in this mess."

He rattled the chains tied to one of the bodies. "Oh your father would have found another way."

"No, he wouldn't," I said, my eyes hunting for my mother "Because he would never have found out about the star to begin with. It was a Foreseer that told him."

"Hmmm ..." Nicholas tapped his lip. "It really does sound kind of pointless. Perhaps one day someone will free all of them and destroy it."

"So where's your mom?" Laylen asked, staring at the bodies implanted with tubes. He leaned forward, getting a closer look. "It's hard to tell who they are."

I shrugged, heading to the left of the crystal. "You wanna take the right?"

Laylen nodded and disappeared around the other side.

"What about me?" Nicholas yelled.

"Do whatever the hell you want." I called over my shoulder. My eyes scanned each person, questioning if Nicholas was just full of it, or if this was just another one of his games.

When we were kids he used to pull crap like this all the time. I'd always hated when he visited the Keepers castle. Everything was a joke to him and he constantly teased Gemma. There was this one specific time when he almost convinced her to go swimming in the lake. That's when I lost it and made a plan to get rid of him. Gemma and I had stolen the *Cruciatus* diamond—the Queen of The Underworld's diamond, and when my father went looking for it, I'd blamed it on Nicholas. My father was so furious he never let Nicholas back into the castle.

And he had been holding a grudge against me ever since. But it was a mutual feeling.

I was about to give up on my search and leave, when I thought I spotted her. It was hard to tell for sure because it had been so long since I last saw her. Her skin was much paler, her dark hair thin, and her head hung lifelessly. I quickly yanked out the tubes and snapped the chains, supporting her weight as she slumped against me.

Her eyes opened and I knew—this time without a second guess—that she was my mother.

"Is it time?"

I assumed she was delusional. "I'll get you out of here. Just hang on."

She clutched onto my arm, her hands bleeding from the tubes. "But it's time right? Time to take Gemma to the Afterlife?"

I almost dropped her on the floor. "You know about that? How?"

"Of course I know about that," she said weakly. "That's what I've been waiting for."

Laylen came running over and flopped her other arm around his neck. Then we led her to the front of the crystal.

"Alana," Nicholas said, nodding his head. "Are you ready to go?"

I glared at Nicholas. "How long have you known she was here?"

"Since I died." He answered with a shrug.

"Because that's when you were supposed to know," my mother said wearily. "Now can we go?"

I balanced my mom and we followed Nicholas. Her feet dragged across the crystal floor, like she was barely alive. Once we got far enough down the hallway, Nicholas took out his little traveling ball.

He raised his eyebrows. "Do I need to ask where we're going?"

"You already know," my mother said. "To Gemma. Take us to Gemma."

I wasn't sure what she knew, but I wasn't going to pry until we were far away from faerie boy.

Laylen went through the crystal first. Then my mother took her turn and I followed, wishing that was it.

"Finally," Nicholas said, dropping into the living room. He put the crystal away and dusted off his hands. "My work is done."

My mother lowered herself into the couch. "Would anyone mind getting me a drink of water?"

I started for the kitchen, but Laylen cut me off. "I got it. You should stay here."

"Thanks." I sat down on the couch, cracking my knuckles.

"Alex relax," she said, patting my hand. "This is how it's supposed to be."

"Why were you down there?" I asked.

"Because it's where I was supposed to be," she explained, cleaning some blood off her arm. "Waiting for the day you came to find me, so I could take Gemma to the Afterlife."

I hated being out of the loop, but with this I definitely was. "But how did you know that's what you're supposed to do? It just doesn't ... it doesn't make any sense to me."

"It doesn't have to make sense to you." She rested back and her eyes drifted shut. "It just has to happen. It's the way it works, Alex. Everything that's happening is because of the vision."

I ran my hands through my hair and grinded my teeth. "Why does it always come back to the visions?"

"Because it has to." She sighed. "Visions are our pathways through life. And there had to be one told where we all ended up here, at this very moment, otherwise we wouldn't be here."

"I have no idea what you're trying to say," I said. "I mean first we're told that a vision was tampered with and Gemma needed to fix it. And now you're saying that a vision led us all here."

"Because it did," she said. "There isn't just one soul vision. If there hadn't been another one, Gemma would have never changed Julian's mistake."

"So what? Some Foreseer just went and found a vision where it would all work out."

"Kind of." She yawned and opened her eyes.

I scratched my head. "It still doesn't really make sense."

"Not everything does." She sighed. "Life is very confusing and sometimes things happen that don't make sense."

I eyed her over, her cut skin, her worn-out eyes. "Are you a Banshee?"

"I have to be so I could take Gemma to the Afterlife when the time was right," she said. "I think you'll agree

173

with me that no Banshee is going to let anyone cross over without collecting something for themselves?"

"But why the City of Crystal?" I asked. "I mean, what the heck did you do to end up down there?"

"I didn't do anything. I was hiding. I knew your father would never come looking for me there and no Foreseer would *see* me there. It was my safe place, so I could still be here when the time was right."

"But how do you know all this?"

"How does anyone know anything about the future?"

Foreseers. Always Foreseers.

"Okay, so answer this question." I leaned back against the arm rest. "Why Gemma? Why does it always have to be her?"

"I already told you why," she said impatiently. "It was all part of the vision to save the world. She's the one whose soul was detached, the one with the Foreseer power, the one who changed the vision back, the one who will go to the Afterlife and free the souls that died during this massacre." She let out a breath. "Then she'll go with you to the lake and kill the star. The portal won't open; Stephan, Demetrius, and all the Death Walkers will be killed. And life will go on."

"And what about me?" My voice was sharp over her casual attitude. "What's my purpose?"

"To protect her, to carry the other half of the star, to be there for her—to be her other half."

"But I wasn't there for her," I snapped. "Not when she really needed me." I jumped to my feet, my temper fuming. "And this is such bull. You sit there and say all this like it was her destiny. You knew, so why not just stop it."

"Her father knew, but he'd already learned the hard way that you can't play with life," she said, her voice softening. "You can shift the future however you want it."

"This isn't fair." I shook my head. "There's got to be a way around it."

"There is no other way. The portal is opening, unless the star dies."

I stopped breathing. "What?"

She stood, her legs unsteady. "Have you ever wondered why Stephan was so focused on you two, but not Aislin, Laylen and Aleesa? Because their part wasn't as important. Malefiscus has the power of the star in him too."

I shook my head like a moron who didn't want to believe what was right in front of his eyes.

"Alex," she said. "There are three ways this could go. Either Stephan can bleed you two out, mix your blood with Laylen, Aislin, and Aleesa, and free everything inside that portal. Or you can run and hide, let the portal touch down, Malefiscus will be trapped, but every Death Walker that's ever existed will come out. Or you can destroy the star, destroy Malefiscus, and destroy the portal all at once."

"This is … this is." I was too frustrated for words. "So what you're basically saying is no matter what, the portal's going to open."

"But if you destroy the star, just like Gemma saw you do, then with Malefiscus inside it—there will be enough energy to end everything, including Stephan and Demetrius and every Death Walker."

"This isn't fair." I cursed, ready to explode.

"Alex, sometimes life isn't. Sometimes people have to endure horrible things, while others don't. It's just how life works. You can't control everything."

"That's only part of the reason why I'm pissed off." I was yelling now, but I didn't really give a shit at the moment. "I'm pissed off because you sit here and talk about life and how it's hard. Well, tell that to Gemma, who's never had a life. She spent most of it dead, with no memories, no emotions, no nothing. So tell me, how is that just a hard life."

She had no answer and I stormed up the stairs before she could come up with another explanation. I dropped my head against the wall. Just once, couldn't someone please surprise me in a good way? Tell me some good news. Tell me something that wasn't so freaking complicated.

I let out a breath and realized someone was crying. The bedroom of Marco and Sophia's room was opened and I hurried toward it, my hand edging for my knife. But it wasn't an intruder, it was Gemma, curled in a ball, with her wings wrapped around herself.

"Gemma." I knelt down beside her. "What are you doing?"

Her body tensed and she squirmed, trying to smear all the tears away, before she peeked out of her wings.

"Did something happen?" I glanced around at the bits of paper on the floor. "Where's Aislin?"

"She's stealing a witch's power." She sat up, picking at her feathers. "I'm just waiting for her to come back."

My eyes wandered to the pieces of paper. "What is that?"

She flicked one of the pieces. "My birth certificate." She stood, rubbing her eyes. "Did you find your mom?"

"Yeah. She's downstairs."

She perked up a little. "What did she say? Does she know how to help us?"

Know how to help us? Of course she did, because apparently that was what she'd been waiting around to do. "Yeah, she's got a plan and everything."

"Good, I'm glad someone finally does." Her eyebrows furrowed. "Is there something else? You seem ... I don't know, a little bothered."

I shook my head, rubbing my thumb between her brows, erasing the worry. "No, everything's fine." And I wasn't lying to her. Like my mother said, my life was made to protect her. And that's exactly what I would do, until I took my last breath.

And maybe even after that.

Chapter 31
(Gemma)

He was acting strange. And the electricity was offbeat and it was making me offbeat. I considered asking him what was up, but knew he probably wouldn't tell me.

We went downstairs and his mother, Alana, didn't seem that shocked by my wings. In fact, she didn't seem shocked about any of this. But maybe Alex had already told her everything.

Laylen was there too, both of them staring at each other from across the room, like they didn't know what to do with themselves.

"So are you ready to go to the Afterlife," Alana said, getting straight to the point. She looked like Alex, at least in the eyes, the same shade of bright green. "Although, we should get the wings off you first."

"Where's Aislin?" Alex glanced at the clock. "Shouldn't she be here? I mean, how long does it take to steal a witch's power?"

"She has …" I checked the time. "Nine minutes left."

"Nine minutes?" He flopped down on the sofa. "That's precise."

I slid down next to Laylen, putting space between Alex and myself, because his weird vibe was making me tired. "I gave her a time frame and if she' not back by then, then I go looking for her."

"Couldn't she do it from here?" Laylen kicked his feet up on the coffee table. "There's plenty of witches outside."

I adjusted my wings. "No, apparently, witches aren't nice about getting their power stolen, so she wanted to make sure they couldn't track down where she lived."

Laylen bit at his lip ring. "Is she in danger? I mean, it sounds dangerous. Maybe we should go look for her."

I looked at the clock again. "We can if she's not back in seven minutes. That was our deal."

We all sat quietly, listening to the clock ticking.

"I hate to interrupt a good time," Nicholas's voice whooshed through the room. "But I'd just like to mention that you owe me my life."

"Excuse me," I said, my eyes searching for him. "I don't owe you anything."

"How can I hear him?" Laylen asked. "I don't have the ring on."

"It's a Banshee thing," Alana said with a sigh. "We have a ghostly connection and I'm channeling it through all of you."

"But we still can't see him?"

"Do you really want to?" Alex asked and pointed to the side of Laylen. "And he's right there."

I felt Laylen shift toward me. "You could have mentioned that earlier."

"I'm sorry," I said, staring at the empty space Alex pointed at. "But why do you think I owe you your life."

"Because Alex made a bargain in your name." Nicholas giggled. "It was so nice of him."

I gaped at Alex. "You did *what*?"

"It was the only way I could get him to tell me where she was." Alex nodded at his mother and then shot a glare in Nicholas's direction. "You know how he is."

"Okay, but how's Gemma even supposed to do that?" Laylen asked the question I was thinking. "Because I'm really curious."

"She'll make sure to include his name when she makes the bargain with Helena," Alana chimed in, like she'd known this all along.

"So I'm going then?" I asked her. "You're going to help me."

"Alex." Alana turned to him. "Give Gemma the ring back."

He slid his hand to the side of him and hid it under his leg. "No way."

"Alex." Her voice was calm, but firm. "She needs the ring to enter the Afterlife."

He scoffed, almost yanking his finger off as he removed the ring. Then he slapped it down on the coffee table, where it spun like a top, finally landing on its side, the violet-gem directed at me.

I put the ring on and Nicholas appeared. He winked at me and gave a mocking wave in front of Laylen's face.

Laylen leaned into me. "How close is he? He's not touching me is he? Because I'm starting to find this whole ghost thing a little creepy."

"Your fine," I lied.

"*Bzzzz*," Nicholas murmured and Laylen flinched. "Times up."

My eyes darted to the clock and I hopped up.

"What's wrong?" Alex was on his feet, like he was ready for battle

I pointed at the clock. "Aislin's time just ran out. I need to go find her."

Alex caught me by the elbow. "Hold on a sec. You can't just go running off, when a witch fight might be going down."

I shook his arm off, but he wrapped his arms around me, pinning me against him. "I have to. She might be in trouble."

"Then I'll go," he said. I started to open my mouth to argue, but he covered it. "I'll go this time." His voice was slow—pressing.

I bit at my lip, his breath warm on my neck. "You can't get there. I have to take you."

"I'll take him," Nicholas offered, raising his hand.

"Thanks. But no thanks," I said. "You'd probably end up dropping him into the ocean or something."

"He can take me," Alex interrupted.

I hesitated. "Are you sure? Because I wasn't really joking about the ocean thing."

"Yeah, I'm sure." He released me and reached for the ring. "Can I—"

Poof.

I whirled, bumping my elbow into Alex. "Aislin." I breathed relief. "You made it."

She grinned. "Of course I did." She waggled her finger. "And I got the power. So let's get those wings off you." She turned to Alex. "I need you to..." Her mouth fell open. "Mom?"

Alana looked like she was going to cry and she hugged Aislin tight. Then she reached around and pulled Alex in, even though he acted standoffish. I backed away with the slamming realization that I would never have this.

"Wait a minute." I reeled to Nicholas. "Where's my mom?"

He didn't have to say anything. I knew it was bad. Because when someone like Nicholas looked sad, there was no way it could be good.

Tears threatened to fall from my eyes. "She's gone, isn't she?"

He pressed his lips together, nodding, not daring to speak.

183

My lips trembled, the prickle surfacing and stabbing violently at my neck. I didn't say a word, because I couldn't. I left the room, going up to mine, and sank down onto my bed. I hugged a pillow to my chest, letting the tears stream out.

A knock sounded at my door. Before I could answer, Laylen entered. He didn't say a word as he sank on the bed and wrapped his arm around my shoulder.

"I'm sorry," I sniffed, wiping my eyes. "I know it's stupid. I mean, I already thought she was dead once."

"I remember when my parents died," he started after a deep breath. "It hurt so bad I didn't know how to deal with it." He paused. "I kept wishing for time to stop so I didn't have to go through life without them. But it kept moving, despite all my wishing. After a while, the hurt became less painful. I won't lie, though, it never fully goes away. There will always be pain. It just gets easier to carry."

I nodded, tears pouring and I didn't even try to stop them. "And how did you get to that point ... where it became a little easier."

"Time," he said.

"But how much time?"

"As long as you need."

Then he stayed silent, while tears poured down my cheeks, landing on everything below me and marking it with my sorrow. I would never see my mother again. I would never get to know her. I would never have memories of her that didn't include the world ending.

She was gone.

And I had to move on somehow.

But not yet.

No, right now I needed a little more time.

Somehow I fell asleep. When I woke up I felt much lighter. Not in terms of my mourning, but in the sense that my body felt much lighter because my wings were gone. I stared back at the empty space behind me, relieved I no longer had to pack them around. My clothes were back to normal too, which was just about as lovely as the wings being gone.

"Aislin took them off while you were asleep." Alex's voice startled me and I bolted up, blinking against the darkness. He was sitting in the computer chair, skimming through my music. "So long, Good-bye" by 10 Years flowed from the speakers. "Aislin thought it might cheer you up a little if you woke up and they were gone." He swiveled the chair. "Are you ... are you okay?"

"No," I admitted honestly. "But I don't think I'm supposed to be."

He nodded, understanding. "No, I don't think it's that simple is it."

I climbed out of bed, stretching my arms and legs. "I guess I should get going. I've got souls to save."

"Gemma," he started. "Maybe you should—"

"Is your mom ready?" I cut him off, wanting to free the souls that died and eliminate some of the death in the world. "And does she know how I'm getting in there? Does she just walk me to a place?"

He swallowed hard, avoiding my gaze. "The Banshee in Iceland wasn't lying about that part. You have to be dead, so Helena will accept your entry."

"With poison?" I asked and he clicked the computer mouse over and over again. I placed my hand on his, our skin a nip of static. "Is it with poison?"

"It is, unless you choose not to go."

"I have to," I said. "I already said I've got souls to save."

"You don't have to do anything." He rotated in the chair so he was facing me and electricity surged as he placed his hands on my hips. I stepped back, but he pulled me to him. "We could leave. Just you and me. Run away and never look back."

"And what?" I asked. "Just let the world end? Could you do that?"

He pressed his lips together. "Could you?"

"Alex." My voice was soft as I put my hands on his shoulders. "It's time to end this."

He moved his hands away and I turned for the door. "Are you coming?"

He sighed and I heard him shift as he stood up. Then we walked out, side by side, to go take my life.

Chapter 32

(Alex)

It hurt me to see her like that. She was hurting in ways she didn't know how to deal with. And I didn't know what to do. I could have gone to her myself, but I was the one who still had a mother. So I sent Laylen, even though it killed me, because I knew he could help her through it.

And now I was the one helping her to her death.

Gemma held the vile of poison between her finger and thumb, staring at the clear liquid. "So this is what's going to kill me, without actually harming me?"

My mother leaned forward from the sofa and took the vile from her fingers. "It will once Aislin seals it with the Kiss of Death."

It sounds like something straight out of Shakespeare," Gemma remarked, tilting her head, studying the vile.

"Like Romeo and Juliet," Nicholas commented. "Only let's hope this one over here doesn't pull a Romeo and take his own life. Then you'll both be dead."

"Does he really need to be here?" I asked. "It seems kind of pointless."

"We need his help with something," my mother said, cupping the poison in her hand.

"Help with what?" I asked. "Have you actually talked to him?"

"I'd like to point out that I'm staying," Nicholas's voice interrupted. "I'm not going anywhere until my life returns to me."

"But how am I going to get Helena to give up the Lost Souls?" Gemma asked. "Because I don't think she's just going to hand them over."

"With that." My mother taped the ring on Gemma's finger. "That belongs to the queen."

"The last time we tried to make a bargain with a jewel," Gemma frowned, "it didn't work out so well. We ended up trapped in The Underworld with a pissed off queen."

"That won't happen," my mother said. "As long as you're still tied to the human world, the queen can't hurt you. And she'll want that ring more than anything."

Gemma twisted the ring on her finger. "Why? What's so special about it?"

My mother's eye lit up in an inhuman way. "Because inside that ring is her soul."

"Who's soul?" Gemma and I asked.

"The queen's soul," my mom answered, stepping toward Gemma. "That's why you can see the dead when you wear it."

I stepped between them. "There's one thing that is really bugging me about this," I said. "Actually, there's more than one, but this is the biggest. How is she going to come back? How will she start breathing again?"

"That's what you're for." My mother patted my shoulder. "You're part of her in every way, through the promise, through the star, through your soul."

"Soul?" Gemma gave me a confused look. "Am I missing something?"

"Oh." My mother averted her eyes, realizing I never told Gemma that our souls were connected. "All you have to do is revive her when it's time."

"So how do I know when that is?" I asked. "Because I won't know what's going on down there."

Her gaze locked on a space of air. "Nicholas is going to tell you when it's time."

"No freakin' way," I said, wondering if being locked up in the City of Crystal had messed with her head. "You actually want to leave someone like him in charge of something like that."

"It's the only way," she said. "He's the one who can see into their world."

I crossed my arms. "Why can't you just come back?"

She got a look in her eyes I didn't like. "Once I cross over into the Afterlife, I can't come back."

189

"What!" I exclaimed and Gemma gasped.

"I've been avoiding my duties as a Banshee," she said. "Once I turned, I got myself sentenced to the Foreseer's crystal to keep my whereabouts hidden. But now ... when I go there, Helena can make me stay if she chooses to."

"You have to come back," I muttered. "It's ... I ..."

"I will one day." She patted my head like I was still two-years-old. "It's not good-bye forever."

"There's got to be another way," I said, determined that there was. "Maybe Nicholas could take me to the Afterlife."

"Only a Banshee can carry a Lost Soul to the Afterlife." She sank down on the coffee table tucking her hair behind her ears. "And Gemma's the one that's going. I've already explained this."

"Maybe we could find another Banshee then," Gemma suggested, biting at her nails.

"We can't," I answered for my mom. "No other Banshee will bring your soul back."

This was so stupid. Both of them were exactly the same, throwing their lives down like it didn't matter, like they were worth nothing.

"Now that everyone understands their job." My mother stood. "Should we get started?"

"You know," Gemma said, lying on her bed, her hands overlapped across her stomach as if she was preparing her

190

body for death. "In the dream I had—the one where I died—Nicholas was the one that appeared to me."

"That's because you secretly have the hots for me." He rolled around in the computer chair, but without his body, it was just a chair moving on its own.

"Or maybe she just feared it'd be you," I said, from the other side of the room because apparently the electricity would keep the poison from working. And when she actually took it, I was going to have to clear the room altogether, something I was really struggling with.

"Or maybe it's because she can't stop thinking about me." The chair spun in a circle.

"Or maybe it's because for three straight weeks you wouldn't leave me alone," Gemma said, her eyebrows furrowing. "I mean, you were watching me day and night, even when you shouldn't have been."

She pressed her lips together as Nicholas let out a laugh.

"Say whatever you want," he said. "He can't hurt me."

It took me a minute to catch on. "Wait. Was he ... when you say watching ..."

"Yes," Aislin said shaking the vile. "We all know Nicholas is a pervert. Now will you all shut up so I don't mess this up? It's important."

I sealed my lips and leaned back against the wall.

"Okay." Aislin sat down at the foot of the bed. "I need complete silence." She waited until the house was hushed.

191

"*Signa hoc venenum cum osculum vitae,*" she whispered, swishing the liquid. "*Servare quicumque bibit spirans. Sed signa voluntas osculum mortem et eorum cor mittimus.*" The vile bubbled, morphing to a shade darker than black. "Now, that's death."

"Is it time to go?" My mother entered the room.

Aislin showed her the vile. "We're all set."

My mother nodded. Aislin ran over and hugged her. "This isn't good-bye," my mother whispered. "I'll be back one day."

Aislin pulled away, rubbing the tears from her eyes and nodding.

Then it was my turn. She pulled me into a hug and it almost popped my lungs.

I cleared my throat as I backed away. "You better come back."

"I'll do my best." She turned. "Gemma, I'll meet you there." Then she was gone, as quick as she'd arrived, like a mere visit from a ghost.

I was sadder than I expected. A rush of emotion overcame me, making me uncomfortable. I cleared my throat hard and tried to gain composure.

"Are you ready?" Aislin asked Gemma.

Gemma nodded and took the vile from her hand. "As ready as I'll ever be."

Aislin looked over her shoulder. "You need to go downstairs."

I pressed my lips together, stepping for the bed.

But Aislin held up her hand. "You can't be near her at all. She needs to be calm."

I locked eyes with Gemma and thought of our Forever Promise, made one dreary day, when two kids were trying to hold on to something that might never be again. And it was like she understood, like she knew what I was thinking. She touched the scar on her hand.

It was one of the hardest things, walking away, leaving that room, knowing she would breathe her last breath.

But I left, just like I was supposed to.

When I walked into the kitchen, Laylen was there messing around with the pipes under the sink.

"You're not going to see her before she ..." I trailed off, not bothering to even try to say it.

He focused on twisting a bolt. "I can't ... it's too ..."

I nodded, rolling up my sleeves. "So you need any help."

He shrugged. "Sure."

I reached for the wrench, feeling her slipping away as she died.

Chapter 33

(Gemma)

I watched him leave, his eyes sad, his muscles tense as he forced them to move. He took the electricity with him, along with some of my soul apparently. When I returned, I'd press him for the details.

I clutched my hand around the vile, letting out a hefty sigh. "So this is it? The Kiss of Death."

"Don't worry," Aislin assured me from the foot of my bed. "You'll come back."

I knew I would. After all, I wasn't finished with life quite yet. I had seen what was going to happen with my future. And since I hadn't been able to change it, as far as I was concerned, my life was over. Alex and I would go to the lake and take our own lives, along with Stephan, Demetrius, and every Death Walker on this Earth.

"I wonder how it tastes?" I examined the bottle as it bubbled. "Because it looks really gross."

"It probably tastes gross," Aislin said. "I'm sure death can't taste good."

"Well." I raised it in the air, like I was making a toast. "Here's to coming back to life and freeing the souls." Then I kissed my lips to the rim, tipped it back, and swallowed. "You're right …. It doesn't taste ..."

My limbs went numb, my heart silencing. I fell back on my bed, into my soul, absorbed by the darkness of death.

When I opened my eyes, I was standing in a field, the breeze a soft lull as it skipped across the grass. Crows circled above me like death and I thought of my nightmare. Then they dove for me and I shielded my head. Their beaks clipped my hair and hands.

"Stop it!" I cried out at the madness and they scattered like mice. I lowered my hands, breathing relief. But where was Alana?

I noticed that one crow lingered behind, soaring in loops, like it was dancing. Then it flipped directions, flapping its wings, and headed off into the unknown. I shoved my way through the tall, dry grass, making a path as I chased after the crow. With every step I took, the crow flew further and then it curved up, becoming just a spot in the sky. I trampled through the field until I broke through to grassless land. There was a house, ancient and damaged, the wood singed with traces of a fire.

I climbed up the front porch and opened the door. Suddenly, I was standing in the same house that was in Iceland, surrounded by charcoaled wall paper and a floor stained with ash.

"Hello," I called out and the door slammed shut. I whirled, yanking at the doorknob.

"Gemma." The sound of her voice was like fresh air.

I turned to Alana. "I wasn't sure if I was in the right place."

She smiled, stretching her hand to me, her bright green eyes welcoming. "You're not quite there yet, but almost."

I took her hand and she led me up the stairs, my body strangely lighter with each stair. I felt a weight rising off my chest, one I hadn't known I was carrying and everything started to make sense, like the pieces of the puzzle had finally connected.

"We're going to die," I said, calm and composed, my head clearer than ever, as if the poison I drank had been filled with knowledge. "Alex and I—we have to, don't we? Otherwise, there's no getting rid of the star or Stephan and everything that comes with him. It has to happen that way, because it's the only way."

"The portal will open regardless," she said, nodding. "But the death of the star will kill it and everything in it."

"Is there any other way?" I wanted to make sure. "A way where I could at least save him?

"You'd do that?" Her hair drifted across her face as she turned her head to me, astonished. "You would save him and let yourself go?"

It was like my life flashed through me, my mind trying to reach unreachable memories. A month—maybe even a week ago, I would have said I didn't know. But now, in my death, it was different. My eyes were finally opened from a life of blindness.

"I think so," I said as we stopped at the top of the staircase in front of a solid black door.

"Hold onto that thought for a while." Alana gripped the doorknob. "Right now, you need to focus on the queen."

"Because it's not as easy as you said it was going to be," I said, knowing there was difficulty before me.

She swung the door open. "Nothing's ever easy, Gemma. Even in death."

And death it was. The air was so thick it suffocated the light, replacing it with a darkness so heavy I nearly buckled to the floor. The foulest smell touched my nose, like the stench of something rotting. I gagged, feeling like I was floating yet falling.

"Keep your head down and try not to look at them," she whispered and then vanished through the doorway.

I tipped my chin down, my hair a curtain around my cheeks. I tried not to breathe the intoxicating air and that's when I realized my need for air was gone. It was the most fascinating thing and that's where I fixed my attention. But then I glimpsed a bony foot in my peripheral vision and I couldn't help it. I peeked between the slivers of space in my hair. They were like mummies, pail and frail, with no meat on their bones, eyes as hollow as their coffins. I told myself to shut my eyes, but I was too fixated on the dead. The tortured. The lost.

"Some of the souls you're here to save," Alana explained over her shoulder. "But don't look at them. It'll upset Helena."

Lovely. I hurried to catch up with her. "How's it going to be harder? Is the queen going to want more than the ring?"

"No, you'll understand soon. And Gemma, whatever you do, don't give her that ring until you've sealed the promise for the freedom of the Lost Souls that were lost because of the mark."

"Will she know what I mean when I say that?" I asked, shutting my eyes as one of the souls let out a sharp cry. "Does she know why I'm here?"

"She's the Queen of the Afterlife," she whispered. "Not the Ruler of the City of Crystal."

I dared another glimpse at the souls, secretly looking for one that looked like my mother, hoping I wouldn't find her.

"She's not here." She ducked her head as the ceiling dipped down "And be grateful she's not."

We reached the end of the tunnel and I suddenly understood what Alana meant. These weren't just Lost Souls,

198

they were tortured souls. The room pulled at my memories of The Underworld, where the Water Faeries tormented those who were sentenced there. This place was the same; bones breaking, painful cries, as the mummy-like bodies were forced to work by men with whips and daggers.

But the difference between The Underworld and the Afterlife was that these souls weren't evil.

They were lost.

Chapter 34
(Alex)

"So we fixed the sink." Laylen leaned back against the counter and folded his arms. "Now what?"

I contemplated this, trying not to think about Gemma, upstairs lying dead in her bed. "Unless there's something else broken, I don't have a damn clue."

"I'm pretty sure we only made the sink worse." He stared at a pool of water on the floor next to his feet.

"What were we even trying to fix?" I asked, not even attempting to hide the fact that I knew zero about plumbing.

Laylen shrugged. "I don't know, I just thought it looked funny."

"That's probably why we couldn't fix it then." I dropped down in a chair, scooting the tools out of the way, and rested my head on the table.

"So who wants to help?" Aislin asked, her cheerful voice like a knife to my ear.

"Go away," I mumbled. "If you're going to be cheerful."

She prodded my side with her foot. "Stop being a downer. I need your help."

"With what?" Laylen asked. "Wait. Let me guess. A spell."

"With removing your Mark of Immortality."

I raised my head, glancing at Laylen, who was staring speechlessly at Aislin.

"You've figured out how?" I asked her. "When?"

She shook her head, frowning. "I'm not sure if I'm quite there yet, but I'm close enough that I want to test it."

"On me." Laylen raised his eyebrows.

She nodded energetically. "Then after I've perfected that, it's on to the shield removing spell. Of course, I'm not sure how I'm going to figure out if that one works ... well, unless I went to Stephan and used a spell on him."

"That's not happening. No one's ever going to be around him again. It's too dangerous," I said. "Hold on ... Why didn't anyone give up our location when you guys switched sides?"

"Because I put an *interpres incantatores* on us," she said. "When you left you missed out on all the amazing things I did." She put her hands on her hips. "I put the spell on the five of us to prevent anyone from telling an enemy our location." She glanced at the boarded window. "And we have a lot of enemies."

"But why didn't you do the spell on me."

She raised her hand in front of her. *"Non proferre verbum ad emeny."* Then she sparked silver dust all over me.

"Dammit Aislin!" I jumped to my feet, dusting off my jeans. "What was that crap?"

"That was the spell," she said and Laylen laughed, thinking she was funny or something. "I'm getting good at this witch thing, huh?"

"Hopefully good enough to even remove the Mark of Immortality." I brushed the last of the silvery stuff off.

"Oh, I am." She dropped a book on the table and opened it to a marked page.

I raised my eyebrows at her. "What's that?"

"A spell book." She said in a *duh* way.

"Sorry I'm not more up to date with my witchcraft knowledge," I said, shoving her hand out of the way. *"Bonum et malum.* What is that?"

"It's the Good and Evil spell." She turned the book, sat down, and Laylen joined us. "It separates the good from the evil."

"But the Mark of Immortality isn't a good thing." Laylen covered the Mark of Immortality on his arm. "So trying to take it off Stephan? That's bad and bad."

"That's not what this is." She tapped her finger on the page. "This spell separates things that don't go together. Like Stephan and the Mark of Immortality. Or like Laylen and his mark."

"It seems like a long shot." I crossed my arms on the table. "Can't you just use the same spell you've been using to take off the Mark of Malefiscus?"

"Magic doesn't work like that." She turned the page. "Everything works according to rules. And as a witch, I think this will do it. There's just one tiny little problem."

I flopped my head back and sighed. "And what's that?"

"There's this thing about blood." She flipped the page back. "It needs the blood of someone who's both good and bad. So any ideas?"

I had one idea, but I wasn't about to say it. If I'd learned anything, it was never to mention this particular person's name in reference to something bad.

"I have an idea." Laylen paused. "Me."

Glad he was the one who said it.

"You what?" Aislin asked, puzzled.

"Me, as in my blood." He stared at the table, ashamed.

"Oh, I don't think that's what it means," Aislin said, skimming the pages with her finger. "It couldn't be …"

"Why not?" I decided to put my two cents in. "He's a vampire and a Keeper. Good and bad, well at least the Keeper part is kind of good."

"Alex," Aislin started.

"No," Laylen put his hand over hers. "I think it might work, if that's the spell you want to try."

She blinked dazedly at his hand and I rolled my eyes. "I don't know. I mean, I guess it might work."

"Alright then." I rubbed my hands together. "Let's do it."

"It more complicated than that, Alex," she said. "We need more than just blood."

"What else do you need?" I heaved a dramatic sigh. "Ice from an Iceberg, salt only from the sea? Or how about the toe of a faerie?"

"No, nothing like that." She paused and then smiled skillfully. "And besides, if we needed the toe of a faerie we wouldn't have a problem. We've got one upstairs."

"That one's a ghost."

"But not for long."

I hated the direction of this conversation. It forced me to think of Nicholas up there with Gemma. "So what else do we need?"

She ran her fingers along the list of ingredients. "Honestly, the worst thing is the blood. Other than that, I probably have most of these things. And anything I don't have can be picked up from a basic witch store." She scooted back from the table. "I'll go check and see what I got."

"She's crazy," I muttered, shaking my head.

"She's your sister." Laylen muffled a laugh.

"And she's your what?" I questioned. "Because I'm still not clear on that."

We stared each other down. He knew what I was thinking, and it was a thought that had crossed my mind more than once. Gemma and Laylen had this close connection and I was never exactly sure what it meant. Were they just friends? Or did he like her more than that?

"That's really none of your business." He rapped his hand on the table and stood up. "I think I'll go help Aislin."

The stillness of the kitchen wore on me quickly. It was driving me crazy not knowing what was going on. Not knowing if everything was going smoothly.

Not knowing if she would make it back to me.

Chapter 35
(Gemma)

"This was worse than I expected," I told Alana. We'd put the torture chamber far behind us and I was happy for a brief moment, before realizing the sights of that room would haunt my dreams for a long time.

"You expected less?" She gestured at the decaying walls, lit up by red lanterns. "This is death Gemma."

"I know," I said. "But I guess I didn't really look at it like that until now."

"When people die before their time," she traced her hand along the wall, "their soul is considered lost. There's no real place for these souls to go, so they end up here. Queen Helena collects them and turns them into the mummies you saw working as slaves."

"But my mom." I swallowed hard. "You said she crossed over. So her soul's not here right?"

"No, Gemma. Her death was her time," she explained and we descended to the right wing.

206

"But she took her own life." I ducked below a row of red ribbons that smelled like they'd been dipped in moldy water. "So how was that her time?"

"Because it was," she replied. "Just like when you will save the world. Your mother's life ended when she took her own life to save you. It was her time to go."

"But how did it save me?" I smacked a ribbon out of the way. "She didn't know if she'd lead Stephan to me. She just feared she would."

"No, she knew." She stopped in an archway and I almost bumped into her.

"I'm sorry, but what?" I scooted back. "Are you talking about a vision?"

She nodded. "Otherwise we wouldn't be here."

This had never occurred to me. That another vision existed. But it made sense. "And how does this one turn out?"

"I think you already know the answer to that." She paused. "Gemma, unless the star is gone the world will end." Then she walked away into the darkness and I followed, trying to shove out of my head the picture of Alex and me dead.

I watched her silhouette as I weaved my way to the mysterious. When my surroundings opened again, I saw a throne. We were in Queen Helena's chambers. Of course there was a throne. This was always the case with someone in higher power, like it was their declaration. This particular throne was twisted with thorny branches, and the

blood red platform in front of it seemed fitting for someone who collected the Lost Souls of the dead. There were
no mummies in the room, but I swore I could hear them
whisper: *Help me, free me, let us live again.*

"She's not here," I noted.

"Oh, she's here." Alana pointed to the ceiling, where
there was a flat sheet of shining silver rippled with our
voices.

The water warped down, a spiral of shimmer, con-
necting to the throne. It formed a body of a woman, silver
and eyeless, with only lips. And the lips knew how to form
words.

"Quomodo audent intra hic sponte. Ubi non est libertas."

Latin. It was always Latin. Why hadn't I learned to
speak the language yet?

"I've come to turn myself in," Alana called out. "And
she ... well, she would like to make a bargain with you."

"I do not make bargains," the queen said, either
switching to English or I suddenly understood Latin.
"There are no bargains here, only souls."

"And feel her soul Helena," Alana said. "Feel it and
you'll see."

I was so lost.

"She's broken," Helena declared, her mouth a pool of
thick liquid. "Why do you bring her to me? Your first time
in the Afterlife and this is it? A soul, broken and torn. This
soul belongs to another. Take her away. No better yet stay
now that you're here."

208

"I've come to bargain for the Lost Souls," I said in a small voice. "Well, some of them, anyway."

Alana nudged my hand, warning me to keep quiet. "She's the one responsible for your heavy amount of traffic lately."

"Well, too bad for her, I don't just give over my souls!" Helena cried, with a slam of her fist, spurting silver liquid onto the red platform.

"Show her the ring," Alana hissed. "Show her now."

I swiftly raised my hand, showing the queen the purple-gemmed ring.

Helena gasped, shocked. "Where did you get that?"

"Um ... I found it," I said stupidly.

With a swish, the liquid body slithered in front of me. She smelled me, like a dog smells a track. "Who are you? And why does your soul feel unnatural, like venom in my lungs."

At first I thought this was a good thing, that maybe, finally, the soul detachment had saved me instead of ruining me.

"It's invigorating. And I want it." Then, with a dive, she swooped down and sucked me into her body.

I could feel her, dead and lethal, and I wanted out of her. Her skin was like warm water, only polluted and revolting.

"Let me out!" I yelled my voice a thin bubble.

She slinked back to the throne and I could see the desire in her eyes. She wanted to keep me.

And there was nothing I could do to change her mind.

"You can't hold onto her forever," Alana said after hours had gone by. "You know you can't. She's not one of your Lost Souls."

"I can if she offers herself to me." She roared, but she was weakening. "And you know the souls that offer themselves to me are the best kind." She pounded her fist, an unstable queen throwing a tantrum like a child over a piece of candy. And I was the candy. "She can offer herself up! She can offer herself up!"

"Helena," Alana said tired, but patient. "You can't have her and you know it. So let her go and hear what she has to say."

There was a pause, then a rumble. The walls shook and the liquid swelled as she undid her mouth and spat me onto the floor.

I scrambled to my feet. "Really?" I wiped the silver spit, or whatever it was, off my arms, shoulders, and hair. "You couldn't just let me go?"

"You're lucky I let you go." She smeared her lips with the back of her hand. "Now what is it you wanted to offer me? My own ring back? Is that what you're offering? Just that and then I let you go and free all your Lost Souls."

"They need to go back," I told her, standing straight and confident, even though I was a nervous wreck on the inside. "You're not supposed to have them and you know it."

She leaned forward in her thrown. "You don't tell me what I'm supposed to have. This is the Afterlife and I rule it however I want."

Raising my hand, I gave her another glimpse of the ring that contained her own soul. "Not even for this? Are you sure?"

She licked her lips. "If I free them, then you'll hand it over?"

"If you free them and give the life back to a faerie named Nicholas."

"Give back a life." She mimicked, then erupted in laughter. "I have no control over such things."

"Yes, you do." Alana stepped onto the podium. "Through your sister, Annabella."

"I don't have any connection with Annabella or her decisions," she snapped. "And how dare you suggest otherwise."

"Oh, I think you do." Alana strolled to the throne, each step cautious like a soldier approaching an enemy. "I know you want your soul back. You've been stuck in that body ever since you lost it, melting away into a helpless being. And you can't take it from Gemma's hand—I know how it works. Whoever holds that ring owns your soul and can only *give* it back to you."

Helena snarled, but then simmered down. "If I were to talk to Annabella and free this faerie's essence, I'd want to talk to Gemma alone before giving her the Lost Souls and letting her back into the mortal world."

I flashed a panicked look at Alana, shaking my head.

"That is my final offer," Helena said. "Take it or take my soul and leave."

Crap.

Alana's lips parted, but I intervened. "I'll do it. I'll talk to her."

Alana bowed her head. "I'll go then."

"But not too far," Helena purred. "You owe me your time, collecting my souls, just like all humans who make the choice to cross over into the Banshee world. Immortality doesn't come without a price. And you. You've been hiding from your debt for a very long time, ever since I agreed to bleed you with Banshee blood and preserve your state."

Alana lowered her head again. "I know what I owe." Then she backed away, out into the hallway, leaving me alone with the liquid queen.

I couldn't tell if her eyes were on me, but I sensed they were, heavy and withholding. "I know you," she finally said.

"Everyone seems to," I replied with a sigh.

"You're important," she said. "Filled with an essence I've never tasted before. Annabella would be excited to get a taste of you."

"As much as I'm flattered," I said. "I really don't think I want to be tasted."

She let out a reverberating laugh that rumbled at the walls and floor. "You're clever. But I wonder just how far that cleverness has taken you and how far it could take you?"

"I'm not sure I'm following you," I admitted.

"You're freeing these Lost Souls for the purpose that they aren't supposed to be here." Her hands curled around the armrests. "But tell me. Why not free your own soul?"

"I didn't realize it needed to be freed."

"Everyone's soul needs to be freed in some way or another. But yours is different. Yours needs to be freed from the pain that holds you captive."

I touched my heart, unbeating and hollow. "My soul's fine."

"But it won't be," she said, "Not after you die. And you will very soon."

"How do you know about that?" I twisted the ring on my finger.

"How do any of us know anything," she said. "Because we choose to."

I wondered if the queen had been conversing with a Foreseer recently. "So you think I'm going to die soon?"

"All humans die," she replied. "Your life just ends sooner, with sacrifice. But you won't be alone. You'll die with someone important to you. Someone you wish you could save."

Alex. "Perhaps."

"But you can't save yourself and others from death. At least not without a price."

"What kind of price." I dared a step toward the throne. "Are you saying there's a way to save us?"

"Not us. Only one. Only one can survive. With a simple sacrifice. One for the other. But the question is who will live and who will die?"

Chapter 36
(Alex)

It had been too long. But there was nothing I could do about it. Laylen and Aislin were watching me like hawks, afraid I would do something stupid like barge into Gemma's room and wake her. I probably could have taken both of them down, although Aislin and her magic might have been a match for me.

"Quit fidgeting," Aislin said sifting through her herbs. "You're driving me crazy."

The TV was on and I flipped through the channels, which were all the same: madness, chaos, death. It was depressing. I clicked the TV off and picked up my knife to sharpen it across a piece of metal.

"You're driving me crazy," I retorted. "Just decide already if you have the stuff or not."

"These aren't marked." She opened a baggy and picked through the green flakes. "It takes some time to sort through them."

I dragged my knife down the sharpener. "Where's Laylen? I thought he was going to check on things."

"He barely went upstairs a few minutes ago." She sealed the baggy shut. "You need to relax."

I pointed the tip of my knife at the stairway. "Relax? You know she's dead up there, right? And her spirit's wandering around in the Afterlife."

She shook a baggie and then picked up another. "What is that?"

"You tell me," I said. "I'm no herb expert."

She narrowed her eyes. "Not this." She motioned over her shoulder. "That banging. It sounds like it's coming from the basement."

My eyebrows furrowed. "This place doesn't have a basement."

She sniffed the baggy. "Well, then it's coming from under the house."

My ears perked, detecting a faint noise. "Yeah, what is that?"

I stood, knife out as I headed for the kitchen. When I turned the corner, it was obvious the noise was coming from underneath the floor. I bounced on the tile, searching for a loose one, wondering if there could be a trapdoor. The center stone, right in front of the table, caught slightly. I squatted down, digging at the grout with my knife. It shifted and sure enough, there was a trapdoor.

I contemplated what to do. Who knows what could be down there? Anything really. And how it got there was

216

puzzling. I tapped my knife on the tile and the banging stopped. Frozen in the silence, I heard a voice.

"Hello."

I backed away. "Aislin, could you come in here?"

The tile grinded as it was forced from the rest of the floor. After a second past, a hand appeared out of the dark hole. "Hello."

I almost dropped my knife at the familiar voice.

The person heaved themselves out of the hole. "Alex," the auburn-haired woman said. "What's going on?"

I moved at the terrified woman and dipped my knife, resting it at her throat. "Who are you?"

She blinked wildly, scared to death. "It's me, Sophia, Gemma's grandmother."

I shook my head. "Sophia's dead. You—what are you? A Banshee? A witch?"

"No, no, no." She raised her hands in surrender. "I swear I'm Sophia." She searched helplessly around the kitchen, looking for something that would prove who she was.

"Better hurry," I said, pushing her to her breaking point.

Tears slipped from her eyes. "I don't know what to do."

I felt kind of sorry for her and considered moving my knife back, to let her breathe, when a pan went soaring through the air and smacked the woman straight in the forehead. Her eyes crossed and she collapsed to the floor.

I turned, finding a wide-eyed Aislin, breathing heavily. "What was that? A zombie or something?"

"Zombies don't exist. You know that." I bent down, examining the stranger. A cut on her head trailed blood down her cheek. "No, she's alive. But did you really have to throw a pan at her?"

"I panicked." She came up behind me. "So if she's not a zombie, then what is she?"

I picked up her wrist, checking her arms for marks and then tilted her head, checking the back of her neck. Beneath the collar of her shirt, I spotted the tip of the Keeper's mark.

"I think it might be Sophia," I stated.

"It can't be," Aislin breathed. "I did a Tracker Spell. It said she was nonexistent. And Marco too."

"Well, then something went wrong?"

"How? I never mess up."

I let out a snort and she smacked me in the back of the head.

"Even if it is her," she said. "Why was she down there?"

I shrugged, heading for the hole, wanting to see if anyone else was down there. "When she wakes up, we're going to find out."

The trapdoor was empty and it reeked too, like someone had been down there for a long time, stirring in their own filth. I climbed back up and filled a cup with water. Aislin had left the room.

I bent down over Sophia. "Wake up." I sprinkled some water on the woman's face and she stirred but didn't wake. I patted her cheek, not very gently. I was really curious where this was going to go. Sophia had been missing for months, vanishing without a trace. And suddenly, she showed up a few days before the portal opened. Just a coincidence?

Another splash of water and her eyes opened. "Alex," she croaked, touching her head. "What happened?"

"You jumped out of a hole in the ground," I said simply. "And then Aislin threw a pan at your head because she thought you were a zombie."

She winced as she touched the cut. "A zombie?"

"Yeah, apparently you're supposed to be dead, but clearly you're not."

She eyeballed my knife resting next to my foot and I picked it up. "Choose what you do really carefully. I won't hesitate to kill you, if it comes down to it."

She shook her head. The once perfectionist woman had bags under her eyes, dirt on her clothes, and knots in her hair. "You're just like your father."

My jaw tightened. "That's the kind of thing that's going to get you killed."

"Sorry, but I'm so confused. The last thing I can remember is Gemma vanishing." Her eyebrows knitted together. "And then Aislin and that vampire showing up."

"What," I stammered. "Aislin and Laylen were here?" I cast a cautious glance over my shoulder, making sure we were alone. "When?"

"I don't know." She massaged her temples. "My brain is so foggy. I remember Gemma disappearing, Stephan yelling at me for letting it happen and then he went on this rampage, murdering Keepers. Marco and I were going to run, but then Aislin and that vampire showed up and sealed me in that trapdoor with some sort of magic spell. They said they needed my gift—*Unus quisnam aufero animus*—so I could detach Gemma's soul again when he finally caught her. Stephan came for me once, but I guess she escaped and he threw me back under the house. And he …" She began to sob. "He killed Marco."

"Why didn't you just climb out?" I asked.

"It's a one-way door that can only be opened from the outside." She blubbered.

"And you didn't think about banging on it earlier."

She rolled up her sleeves, showing me a triangle mark on her arm. "This kept me quiet … and I think I have to … I …" As if a sudden energy surged through her body, she lunged for me. With one move of my fist, I knocked her back out again.

"Aislin," I called out, gripping my knife. "I need to talk to you."

She bounced into the kitchen, Laylen at her heels. "How's it going? Did you find out who she was…" She caught sight of the unconscious Sophia. "Oh, not good huh?"

"I think you two have some explaining to do." I aimed my knife at them and they exchanged puzzled glances.

"What's wrong?" Aislin asked.

"She says you two are the reason she was stuck down there," I said. "Can you tell me why she thinks that?"

Aislin scratched her head. "She's lying. She has to be."

"What happened that time you two disappeared?" I asked. "When we were in Colorado. Where were you guys?"

"We told you. We were running from the Death Walkers in Nevada." Laylen leaned against the doorway, crossing his arms, looking perplexed. "That's where we were ... weren't we?"

Aislin's expression twisted. "I don't know."

"You seemed pretty confident when you showed up to save us," I told them, remembering that day at the cabin in Colorado, when they arrived abruptly, almost out of nowhere.

"Well, you seemed pretty confident when you told us the Death Walkers just picked up your dad and left," Laylen countered. "Seems just as suspicious."

"Why are we even arguing about this?" Aislin complained. "It's in the past."

"It's important because we might have a traitor in our midst." I could almost hear my father laughing.

Chapter 37
(Gemma)

She blobbed down the hall, a silver body of fluid, leading me to her sister, Annabella. This place was different, haunting like a whisper of wind. White wisps of ribbon danced around and coiled up the leafless trees that lined the garden we walked in.

"She's going to want something," Helena said. "An essence perhaps, if you have one."

"What exactly is an essence?" I asked, blowing a ribbon from my face.

"A spirit," she answered, smoothing the wrinkles from her body.

"So what's the difference between a soul and a spirit?"

"A spirit is the ghostly form of a person," she replied. "They are still themselves, possess their soul, can walk and talk on their own. It's what happens to humans when they die. And Lost Souls are the ones disconnected from their bodies, the ones that are lost due to a death before their time."

I thought of Nicholas and how he walked the world. "So why torture the Lost Souls?"

"Why does anyone torture anything?" She smiled with her thick lips of silver. "For power."

"But you lost your own soul," I said. "You think you'd be more sympathetic."

"Sympathy is weakness. Something you should keep in mind before you make your decision." She swirled down the path, a shimmer of light in the white sunlight. "You're a powerful girl, I can sense that. But your humanity makes you weak."

"I think you're wrong." I stood tall with confidence. "It's my humanity that makes me strong."

Her lips twitched. "You're a stupid little girl."

"Perhaps," I said. "But maybe not."

We neared the end of our journey. A woman stood beneath a large willow tree, her hair as white as cotton, her lips as red as a cherry, and her eyes sparkling with silver. She watched us approach, her gaze never faltering, her long black dress trailing in the grass.

"Annabella," Helena's voice nipped.

Annabella lowered her head. "Helena, I sensed you'd crossed."

"Of course you did." Helena stretched her body, trying to rise taller than her sister. "You always do."

Annabelle's eyes were kind. "And you've brought someone who wants something from me."

I stepped below the branches of the willow tree. "I've come to ask you for a favor."

"You want me to free an essence." It wasn't a question.

I nodded. "If you would?"

"But why?" She ducked under a branch and stepped in front of me. "Why ask for the freedom of someone you dislike?"

"I don't dislike him."

"But you don't like him," she said. "Yet you're still here in death, asking me to let him live again."

I sighed deeply. "Nicholas ... he isn't that bad. And he's helped me out." It was the partial truth.

"Is that the only reason?" She wanted more.

I let out a breath. "I feel responsible for his death."

"But he's not a Lost Soul," she said. "No one is responsible for his death."

The branches pirouetted, tickling against my cheeks. "Perhaps he should have ended up one."

"Why do you feel responsible for things that are out of your hands?" she asked.

"He died because I exist," I admitted in the secrecy of the branches canopy. "Many people have."

"It's not your fault you exist," she said. "Everyone has a path in life, even the Lost Souls. They're there because they have to be. They're there because they're lost."

"This is confusing." I sighed, swatting a branch away.

"Death always is." Her silver eyes held my gaze powerfully. "You're better than you think you are, Gemma. Your soul is pure, despite what you think." Then she held out her hand, her skin shimmering like glitter. It swirled down, forming an orb in her hand. "Nicholas's essence."

I was hesitant to touch it. "You're just giving it to me?"

She smiled. "Not everything is complicated. Sometimes the answers are right in our hands."

I traced the scar of the Blood Promise, thinking of Alex. "Nothing's ever easy."

"Sometimes it is." She urged the orb at me. "But it's the easy answers that humans question, which only makes it complicated."

"I think I understand," I said, and gently picked up the orb of essence, which was warm in my hand like sunshine.

"Remember," she said. "Not everything is as hard as you think. Sometimes the answers are right in front of us."

I nodded, turning away from Annabella, her words the wisest ever spoken to me. I followed Helena back through the garden, leaving the warmth of the trees behind and we shifted back to the darkness of the world of Lost Souls.

"My sister makes things too easy," she wallowed, pooling her body back onto her throne. "She just hands it over, without any bargains. She's always been the stupid one."

"It's hard to believe she's your sister." I cupped the orb carefully in my hands. "You two are nothing alike."

"That's because she believes in good, which makes her weak."

"And what do you believe in?" I asked.

She smiled vainly. "Myself."

I couldn't help but think of the story of Malefiscus and his brother Hektor. One selfish, the other good. And in the story, good triumphed for the time being. But I wondered how the story would have gone if Hektor had to sacrifice his life to trap Malefiscus in the portal. Would bad have triumphed instead? Or would he have thrown down his life, to save everyone he ever cared about.

"The question you asked me earlier, I have your answer." I approached the throne, not steady with great sureness, but terrified and emotional. Because that's who I was. I wasn't a fearless soldier with a hero complex to save the world.

I was just a girl, doing what I had to do to make things right.

Chapter 38

(Alex)

"A traitor?" Laylen questioned. "Okay, I think you've finally lost it."

"That sounds like something a traitor would say," I replied, my eyes never leaving him.

He stared me down. "You're insane."

"He's not a traitor!" Aislin cried as she finished removing the Mark of Malefiscus from Sophia. "And I'm not either."

"Then why was I trapped in that floor?" We all turned to Sophia as she sat up, blinking. "I don't understand any of this."

"Are you sure about that?" I asked, nearing my knife to her. "Or could your confusion be an act to make us turn on each other, leaving you room to detach Gemma's soul again." I bent down, getting in her face. "Is this a desperate attempt by my father? Did he put you in the floor to get to us?"

"I never wanted to detach Gemma's soul in the first place," she said quietly. "I thought I was doing what was right. I thought I was protecting the world."

"No, you were ending it."

She nodded quickly. "I know that now, but before, what I was trying to do made sense." She clutched onto my arm and I shook her off. "It's your father. He brainwashed me."

"Trust me," I said. "We've all been there."

Something shattered to the floor. "Oh my God."

I turned. The glass cow that was sitting on the table was now headless on the floor and Aislin's hands were shaking.

"What's wrong?" I asked.

"I can't deal with this anymore," she cried. "He's a horrible man who messes with minds and murders innocent people. What if somehow he got into our heads?"

We all exchanged looks, none of us speaking, or trusting, waiting for something unexpected to happen.

"What are we going to do?" Aislin said, stomping her foot.

"The only thing we can." I reeled back to Sophia and grabbed her arm. "Sorry Sophia, but until we know who's in control of their own actions." I pushed her back in the trapdoor.

"Alex, please!" she begged. "You can't do this! I've ran out of food and I'll starve."

I snatched a few bags of chips, cookies, and bread from the cupboard and tossed them into the trapdoor. "That should hold you until we work this out."

"Alex, please don't leave me down here. I—"

I slid the tile over. "Seal that up," I said to Aislin, feeling bad, but drastic times called for drastic measures.

Aislin hurried over, running her finger along the crack. "*Signa eius intus et clauditis hoc usque.*" The tile shimmered, the cracks blending away. She stood to her feet. "Oh no!"

"What?" I asked. "Didn't it work?"

She turned. "I've done that before."

I was about to jump for her, take her down, and tie her up until I could figure out what the hell was going on. But then Nicholas entered, solid, human, and alive. He turned over his arms, incredulous.

"It's time," he said, solemn for the first day in his life.

I shoved past him, knocking him into the wall, and then I charged up the stairs, ready to wake her. She was lying, motionless in her bed, skin paled with death, but just as beautiful as ever. I didn't feel the electricity until I was right beside the bed. The life in her was so weak it was barely a shock of static. I touched her ice-cold skin and bushed her hair back, waiting for her to open her eyes.

But she didn't stir, didn't breath, and I cupped my hands around her face. "Gemma, can you hear me?"

The only sound was silence.

I shook her gently by the shoulders. "Gemma. Wake up."

But her body was limp. "Aislin!" I yelled, trying not to panic. Because I knew better than to panic. But this was pushing me. I inched my mouth for hers.

"Gemma, please." And then I kissed her.

Chapter 39
(Gemma)

When the queen freed the souls, I could hear them whisking away, back to the world, back to their bodies. Then she held out her hand, her mood elated as I placed the ring in her palm.

She slipped the ring on her finger and her body shifted into form. Her skin was like the Lost Souls, mummified and hideous, her hair a grey veil. Her lips were thin and her eyes hollow. She let out a sigh, like she was glad to be back in her own skin. But I didn't know why. She looked better in liquid.

"That's much better." She stretched her arms above her head and grinned. "You can go now. I have what I need."

I nodded and ran as fast as I could, never looking back. Alana was waiting for me in the archway.

"You did it," she said happily, but there was sadness about her too. "Congratulations."

I tucked Nicholas's essence under my arm. "Are you going to be okay? I could try to go back and get her to free you?"

She shook her head. "No, you won't. I'll pay my dues, like I'm supposed to."

"And then what?" I asked. "Will we ever see you again?"

She didn't answer, drawing me in for a hug. "You're an amazing girl, Gemma Lucas. You really are." Then she let me go. "Take care of him for me."

I nodded. "I will." Then I turned down the hall and the light captured me.

When my feet touched ground again, I was back in the grassy field only there were no crows.

"Bout time you showed up." The half-faerie's voice rose over my shoulder. "I thought the queen had killed you or something."

I turned, his essence tucked up against me. "Nope, she let me be." I handed him the orb. "Your essence."

He swallowed hard, no tricky faerie evident in his eyes. In fact, he looked very human at that moment, about to be reunited with his life. He took the orb in his hands, his eyes glowing against the light, tears staining the corners of his eyes. "Thank you."

Two simple words, but coming from him it was a lot.

"You're welcome," I said. "Now can you go tell Alex to revive me?"

He nodded, shoving the orb into his chest. And then, he was gone.

I sat down in the field, picking at the grass, and listening to the wind whisper. I felt different somehow, my mind less heavy, like my eyes had suddenly been opened. Annabella had told me that humans made the easiest things complicated. And she was right. The answer had been in front of me the whole time. There was no loophole for this one, no magic trick that would save me. Either I could go to the lake and end everything or I could stay away and let the world go.

It was that simple.

I shut my eyes, dandelion seeds kissing my cheeks as I was sucked back to my life.

When I opened my eyes, his lips were on mine. Hot and fiery, I wanted to close my eyes again and let him keep kissing me. But the sharp zip of electricity caused him to shudder and he stumbled back.

He let out a huge sigh. "I thought you were dead."

"I was." I sat up in my bed, blinking my eyes.

He shook his head, laughing. But then he remembered. "Are you okay? Did you free the Lost Souls?"

I motioned at the window. "Why don't you go look and see?"

He moved to the window and pried the board off. "You really are amazing," he said, stunned by the sight of the mellow streets. "You know that." Then he turned to me, with this look like he'd suddenly figured out something that frightened him.

I slid my legs over the side of the bed. "So anything exciting happen while I was gone?"

The corners of his mouth curved down. "Yeah, a lot actually. And I'm pretty sure we might need to hide out for a while."

"Hide out from what?" I stood, the wooziness of death still lingering in my head. "We're already hiding."

"Hide out from them." He pointed to the floor. "Aislin and Laylen and … Sophia."

I gasped, my vision spotting.

"Gemma, breathe."

I massaged my temples. "I'm sorry, but I think I just imagined something really weird. Did you say Sophia is downstairs?"

"No, you weren't imagining it," he said slowly. "Something happened."

"Something always happens," I said, giving a nervous glance at the shut door. "But this? This is more than a something."

"Don't worry," Alex said. "She's trapped in the floor."

I sighed. "Why doesn't that surprise me?"

He started to smile, but then suppressed it. "There's more to it than that."

"How much more?"

He sank down in the computer chair. "Sit down and I'll explain."

"So you're saying she's been trapped in the floor this entire time?" My jaw was hanging to my knees. "And that Aislin and Laylen were the ones who put her there?"

"That's the rumor that's going around." He leaned forward in the chair, overlapping his fingers. "But it makes sense. I mean, when Aislin and Laylen showed up at the Hartfield cabin that day, they seemed so confused about where they'd been. And I think my dad brainwashed them temporarily. When the *memoria extracto* backfired on him, I think they might have been freed from him because they showed up right after that."

I choked on a laugh.

He arched an eyebrow. "Care to share what's so amusing?"

"It's just that this whole time I thought you were the one lying." Laughter snuck into my voice. "And it turns out it was Aislin and Laylen."

"I don't think they were lying," he said. "I just think they couldn't remember."

"I know." I wiped some tears from my eyes.

"I don't get why you think this is amusing," he said, trying not to laugh. "This is some serious stuff."

"Oh, I know it is." I flopped back on the bed, lost in my laughter. I knew it was probably inappropriate, but for such a long time, I'd questioned which legion Alex was part of. God, all that wasted energy.

"Well, I'm glad you find this so funny," he remarked.

I sat back up, putting my serious face back on. "Okay, tell me how we're going to fix it. How do we know for sure if they're okay?"

He tapped his finger on his knee, considering. "Honestly, Gemma, I really can't think of anything. Usually for this particular kind of thing, I'd ask Aislin to do a spell or something, but how do we know if she does it right ... and really, it's been so long, I don't think they're still brainwashed."

"And what about Sophia?" I asked. "Are you just planning on leaving her trapped in the floor?"

He stopped tapping. "I was going to let you decide what to do about that. She's the one who ...." He stopped, unable to speak.

"Destroyed my life," I finished for him. "No, I don't really think that was her. I saw her in a vision, when she removed my soul and she looked like she didn't want to, but couldn't seem to stop herself." I paused. "Where's Marco?"

"He's dead," he said quietly. "My father killed him."

"But he didn't kill Sophia." I considered the reason why. "Because she's the only one who could detach my soul again."

"I think so," Alex nodded, agreeing. "So what do we do now?"

"The only thing we can do," I said, a quiver in my voice. "We leave her there until we die."

He was on his feet before I could even finish. "What's wrong with you? You can't be giving up that easy."

"We're not giving up," I said. "We're doing what we have to do."

"So what? You just quit." His words breathed fire in my face.

I shook my head. "No, I'm not giving up. I'm doing what I have to do to save the world."

He dragged his fingers down his face. "There has to be another way."

"No, there's not. And we don't have any time left," I said. "And it doesn't matter. I've known this was going to happen, I've just been making it complicated, when all along the answer was right in front of me." I put my hand on his cheek, a forbidden electric touch. "We die, so everyone else can live."

I touched my lips to his, a quick brush, then walked out the door.

Even though he was angry with my answer, I hoped he would follow me.

And he did.

Chapter 40
(Alex)

I can't believe she really thought that was going to happen; that I was just going to let her give up like that. I followed her down the stairs anyway, but mainly to make sure Laylen and Aislin weren't flipping out.

Everything was quiet, still as death.

Aislin was at the coffee table, mixing a bowl of herbs. "You're alive," she joked with a smile.

"Do you realize how many times you've said that to me," Gemma joked back as if nothing was wrong, as if she hadn't just been dead, hadn't gone to the Afterlife, hadn't announced that she was going to sacrifice her life.

Aislin laughed, crunching leaves and Gemma made a face at the stench. Her eyes wandered over to me, curious if I'd break the news to everyone.

But in my opinion there was no news to break.

"What is that stuff?" Gemma gagged, peering in the bowl.

"This is what's going to take the Shield Spell off my father." She gave the bowl a spin. "Of course, after we do that, I don't know what we're going to do. No one's come up with a plan to end him."

Again, Gemma glanced at me and I shook my head once, warning her not to talk about her stupid death plan.

"So where's Laylen?" she asked.

"Right here," he announced, pushing me aside as he stepped into the living room and gave her hug. "Notice anything different?"

She tucked her hair behind her ears. "Did you get taller?" she teased.

He stuck out his arm and she gasped, tugging it closer to her. "Your mark's gone! You're free."

He shrugged. "Not completely." He grinded his teeth. "But close."

Gemma hugged him again, her eyes meeting mine and I glared at her. She let go of Laylen. "I'm glad you're happy." Then she marched up and took me by the elbow, pulling me into the foyer and out the front door.

"See all this," she said with a swing of her hand.

"Looks like a street." I shrugged, leaning back against the railing. Snow was falling lightly and our breaths fogged in front of us.

"A quiet peaceful street," she said, staring at the houses on the other side of the road. "And it could stay that way."

"I'm not letting you die," I said. "I refuse to. We haven't even ..." God, I sounded like an idiot. I took her by the shoulders, looking her in the eye. "You haven't even lived. I mean really lived, without all of this."

"Death's not that bad." But she winced when she said it.

My hands fell from her shoulders, because my palms were too hot to touch her any longer. I started to speak, but she put a finger to my lips.

"Can I show you something?" she asked, eyes wild with excitement.

I pointed at the house. "Don't you think we should help Aislin with the shield spell?"

She shook her head, hair blowing in her face, her violet eyes eager with something I couldn't understand. "They'll be fine. Aislin will get the spell working."

"How do you know that?" I folded my arms.

She smoothed the hair out of her mouth. "Because I've seen how this is all going to end. The world will be safe. Everyone will be safe." Then she pushed past me back into the house, not waiting to see if I followed. And I wasn't planning on it. I'd stand out here all damn day if I had too, until she could see that I wasn't about to give up.

But this was nothing but a threat to myself I realized. I trailed after her, catching up as she reached the stairs.

"I think I almost got it," Aislin announced, beaming in the doorway of the living room, the bowl resting against her hip as she stirred. Something in our expressions made her back away, like she knew a secret and was giving us our space. It made me wonder what I was about to walk into.

Gemma climbed up the stairs, her footsteps quick. Her hands quivered as she opened her bedroom door. She walked over to her computer and picked up a candle, turning it in her hand.

"This is what I wanted to show you," she said, her voice shaking. She cleared her throat.

"Okay. It's …nice." Was I missing something?

She frowned, disappointed. "It's nice? That's all you have to say?"

"It's a candle." I shrugged. "What do you want me to say?"

She bit at her lip, biting back a smile. "No, it's so much more than a candle."

Chapter 41
(Gemma)

"So what is it then?" he asked, unaware of the importance of this moment.

"It's a candle," I stated.

He rolled his eyes and the corners of his mouth quirked up. "Obviously, Gemma. But what's so special about it." He took the small rainbow candle from my hand.

I grabbed a lighter off my desk and flicked it open. "A witch gave it to me." I didn't bother mentioning what I gave up to get the candle. Without my locket, my neck felt bare and exposed, just like my emotions did now. "It's a Power of Entrapment candle. I got it from the Black Magic place."

He was already shaking his head. "We're not using anything that came from a black magic place. It's too dangerous."

"We already did," I pointed out. "We used a whole bunch of stuff, so Aislin could remove my wings."

His eyes moved to my wingless back. "Yeah, but that was an emergency."

"So's this candle," I said, knowing I was stretching it on the emergency part.

"Okay. Do you want to tell me what it does? Maybe then I can decide for myself whether we want to use it for whatever you're thinking."

I was thinking a lot. At that moment, millions of images flooded my mind, some real, some made up. "It's supposed to trap the power of a witch in her body, at least while the wick burns."

"So you want to use it on Aislin or something?" He asked, utterly baffled. "Because I think that might be a little harsh."

God, did I have to spell it out for him. "I want to—" My voice squeaked and I pretended to cough. "I want to use it to trap *our* power in *our* bodies."

I saw it register in his eyes, like a curtain opening. "How'd you get it?" He pinched the wick.

"I told you, at the witch store."

"I know, but it seems like something that would come at a big price."

I shrugged, forcing down the lump in my throat. "Only dollars from my pocket."

He turned the candle upside down. "And how do we know it works? How do we know it's not going to kill us?"

My hand shook as I flicked the lighter. "Only one way to find out. Are you in?"

He stared me down, his expression never wavering. "I'm in."

Suspending the lighter over the wick, my hand shook as I lit it. Then I jerked back quickly, hoping it wouldn't explode. We held our breaths as the wick burned bright. There was no magical sparks, no enchanting noises or special effects. There was only silence. And the beating of our hearts.

And just like it was supposed to, the electricity of the star sizzled out, momentarily preserved inside each of us, unable to connect.

But it would only be like this momentarily. Like most good things are, as quick as a breath, or a skip of a heartbeat, as swift as our lives would leave us, it would burn out, just like us.

But right now I didn't care. Right now, I only cared about one thing.

"As soon as the wicks gone, it'll stop," I said. "The electricity will come back."

He nodded, bright green eyes hypnotized by the flame. "I know."

Then we locked eyes, taking in the silence, thinking of the possibilities.

***

"This is for Keeps" by Spill Canvas poured from the speakers. The room was dark, night shading the outside. The stars twinkled brightly through my bedroom window. I was lying on my back, Alex leaning over me, his heart knocking against my chest as he kissed the tip of my ear.

"This song's good," he whispered.

"I think it might be about immortality or something," I muttered, my eyelids fluttering as he kissed my neck.

He jerked back slightly. "Where's your necklace?"

My hand touched the hollow of my neck. "I lost it. I think the hook broke or something."

"I'm sorry," he said and then stole another kiss from my lips, which were already swollen from the many other kisses he'd stolen within the last hour. Then he slid to my side, eyes watching me with intensity.

"What?" I asked. "Why are you looking at me like that?

He shrugged. "It's nothing." He followed my gaze as he rolled on his back and took my hand. "Still fascinated with them?"

"The stars?" I shook my head. "No, I was just thinking about something, that's all."

"Care to share your thoughts?" He cocked an eyebrow as he propped up on his elbow.

"I was thinking about death," I began and he immediately frowned. "And about life, and wondering where it will go."

"Where what will go?"

"The star. After this is all over." My eyes were fixated on the stars, shimmering and twinkling. It wasn't there anymore. That pull. Instead it was like a push, like the star was the one holding me down. "Will it go back up there? Or will it just be gone?"

He didn't speak and I figured he didn't like where the conversation was heading. "Did you know that Gemma is an actual star?"

"Obviously," I rolled my eyes.

"No, Gemma, also known as Alphecca, is part of the constellation Corona Borealis." He traced my lip with his finger.

"How did I not know this?" I wondered, rubbing my lips together.

"Because there are a ton of constellations and an endless amount of stars."

"But you know." I wrapped my arms around his waist and ran my fingers up his back, trying not to smile as he shivered. "What'd you do? Google it or something?"

He shot me a look like that was the most ridiculous thing he'd ever heard. "No, I didn't Google it."

The song switched to "Here by Me" by 3 Doors Down.

"You just know all this then?" I asked.

He nodded and then winked at me. "Haven't you figured out I know everything."

He was joking, but I still couldn't help but think how very wrong he was. There was something he didn't know—and would never know.

Because I would never tell him.

Chapter 42
(Alex)

We never left the floor, not wanting to move, afraid the candle might burn out with the slightest shift of our bodies. I kissed her until her eyes shut, until she finally fell asleep in my arms, breathing softly, dreaming of dreams I hoped were good.

The song switched to Spill Canvas's "Lullaby," as the last of the wick struggled to stay lit. I couldn't seem to take my eyes off it as it slowly lost the last of its light. How could we just die? Forget my life, it didn't matter without her beside me. How could I let her die? How could this moment be her one and only moment where she knew something was real? This wasn't how it was supposed to work out. There had to be more.

It was like an epiphany had slapped me across the head and woke me up from a trance. The answer had been staring me in the face for the last few days. My mother had said it; that everything happened for a reason.

She was right.

I slowly rolled over and stood to my feet, watching the candle die. My skin erupted with heat and I knew I had to move fast. I bent down, giving her one last kiss on the cheek and she breathed from the sparks, but didn't wake.

"*Ego amare*," I whispered, the realest words I'd ever spoken. And then I was gone. Returning to the one place that had seemed like such a pointless journey.

Now it was more important than anything.

"I need your help," I announced to Aislin as I entered the living room.

She was lolling on the couch, her feet kicked up on Laylen's lap and she smiled teasingly. "Did you two have fun up there?"

"Shut up," I said. "Could you just come with me for a minute? There's something I need to ask you." My eyes roamed to Laylen. "Alone."

She sighed, got up from the couch, and followed me into the kitchen. "So what's up now? You need me to conjure a spell? Because I'm already working on one in case you've forgotten. A big one."

"I need you to take me somewhere." I let out a breath, preparing for her reaction. "I need you to take me to Iceland."

"W-what?" she stammered. "Iceland? Why? Shouldn't we be coming up with a plan to save you two? I mean, tomorrow is the day."

"I know," I said. "And that's why."

"So you know how to do it?" she asked hopeful. "How to save both of you from dying?"

I took her by the shoulders, looking her directly in the eyes. "Yeah, but I don't save myself."

"No." She shook her head madly. "You can't do that Alex. Don't be stupid."

"I'm not being stupid," I said. "I'm doing exactly what I'm supposed to."

"No, you're trying to be a hero," she snapped. "A stupid hero."

"Aislin, you'll be okay. You've got Laylen and Gemma and mom won't be gone forever."

"But why does it always have to be you." Tears flooded her cheeks.

"It's never been me, Aislin." I let my hands fall to my side. "She's the one that spent most of her life unemotional, with a broken soul. She has no memories of her childhood, no really happy memories that don't have some kind of burden attached to them. She's been tormented by the Death Walkers. By our father. Nothing about her life is fair."

She blinked back the tears. "I know, but yours hasn't been that fair either—none of our lives have been easy."

"And that's why we need to stop all this," I said. "So no one has to suffer anymore."

"Are you sure there's not another way, though? Where no one has to die, except the bad guys?"

I shook my head. "Mom told me that the portal's going to open up no matter what and the only way to seal it back is for the star to die—is for us to die."

She gasped, clutching onto the edge of the counter. "Why didn't you say so? How can you keep things like this from me?"

"What would have been the point of telling you early?" I asked. "It's going to happen no matter what. But I think I know a way to save Gemma."

"But why can't both of you be saved?"

"Because I can't be. What I'm doing ... one of us has to die."

Her breathing was ragged as she sucked back tears. "I'll take you, but I'm not taking you to your death, am I? You're coming back right?"

"Yeah, I'm coming back," I said. "And then tomorrow we finish this. You're going to have to get that shield spell working."

"That's the problem." She frowned, tears still dripping from her eyes. "I thought maybe when I stole the witch's power it would give me enough power to remove it. But it didn't."

251

I paused, contemplating. "I think I know something that might work. But I need to go to Iceland first, okay. This needs to be taken care of."

Our mom had been right when she said it always was Gemma. Because, if I could make this work, Gemma was the one who was going to live.

"I need you to do me favor," I said to Laylen from the living room doorway.

He turned his head from the TV, looking at me oddly. "The last time you asked me to do you a favor, you left."

"I'm leaving, but I'll be back," I said. "I need you to keep an eye on her. I need you to make a Blood Promise with me that you'll always keep an eye on her, no matter what happens."

"Why?" He questioned.

"Because." I rubbed the back of my neck tensely. "It's just important, okay?"

Nodding, he stood up and I switched out my knife. I sliced my palm—the one without the scar of the Blood Promise. Then I tossed the knife to him and he cut his own, his lip twitching at the blood.

"You okay there man?" I asked, cupping my hand.

"Yeah, I'm good." He chucked the knife on the table. "So, can I just point out, that this is kind of awkward?"

"It always is," I said and then we pressed our hands together and it was super awkward.

"So what's the magic words this time?" he asked with a twitch in his hand.

"*Ego spondeo vos ut haud res quis gemma curam et custodiam eam iniuriam,*" I said quietly, wishing I was on the other side of this promise.

He took a breath, suddenly understanding. "*Ego spondeo vos ut haud res quis gemma curam et custodiam eam iniuriam.*"

We broke our hands away and I wiped mine on the side of my jeans. "Okay, we good?"

"We're good." He dabbed his hand on his shirt.

"Am I walking in on something I'm not supposed to?" Nicholas was leaning against the wall, with a mocking expression, back to his normal self.

"You need to leave." I grabbed the collar of his shirt and shoved him out of the room toward the front door.

"Hey, this isn't your house," he argued, trying to plant his feet firmly against the floor.

"Yeah, but I'm eliminating all risk factors right now." I opened the front door. "And you're one of them."

"What? You don't trust me?" He faked offence.

"Nope." I nudged the screen door open with my foot. "Now go."

He stepped out onto the porch, tripping over the threshold. "Is this a temporary thing?"

"I hope not," I said, giving him another shove. "But that's no longer my decision." Then I slammed the door in his face, glad to see the faerie go.

Aislin stepped behind me, tears in her eyes and a reluctant frown on her face. "Are you ready to go?"

"Yep," I said. "Take me to Iceland."

Chapter 43
(Gemma)

"It will be alright," he whispered, brushing my hair back. *"I'll always save you."*

"But I don't want you to save me," I said. *"I want to save you."*

"It can't be that way." The ice crackled over his voice.

"It can if I want it to be," I said my hair blowing in the wind. *"It has to be me. It just has to."*

"No, it doesn't." He leaned close, tracing his finger along my cheekbone. *"It never has to be you again. I'll always save you Gemma, just like I promised."*

I shook my head, holding onto him as the Death Walkers descended from the trees. Their eyes lit with fire. Stephan stood in the middle, his cloak billowing behind him. "Please don't leave me."

The wind howled against my words. Ice laced my breath. My bones chilled.

"I have to," he said. *"This is how it was supposed to be."*

"No." I shook my head. "This isn't how our story goes — this isn't how I saw it."

"Everything happens for a reason," he said. "Even this."

Then he pulled me against him.

"Don't let me go," I whispered.

But as the electricity sparkled, freeing itself from us, we slipped to the earth, our bodies breaking.

Only one of us survived.

When I opened my eyes, I felt hollow and numb. My room was dark. Alex was gone. All the amazing feelings I'd had when I drifted to sleep, had evaporated.

I got to my feet, stumbled across my room, and cracked open the door. The house was silent, except for the sound of the TV. I stepped into the hall and padded down the stairs, finding only one person.

A tall vampire sat with his legs kicked up on the table. He turned his head as if he sensed me. "I was wondering when you were going to wake up."

Outside, the sky was dark, stars twinkling a song I almost knew. "What time is it? And where is everyone?"

"They took off somewhere." He shrugged me off. "They wanted to have some brother and sister good-bye or something."

I slumped down on the couch. "But they're coming back, right?"

"Yeah." His eyes were on the TV screen. "They'll be back."

"You sure?" I asked, crossing my arms. "Or are you just telling me that?"

He met my eyes and they were full of truth. "Yeah, Gemma. They're coming back."

I sighed with relief. "So Alex is finally accepting this, then?"

"What?" Laylen said. "You two dying? I'm not so sure."

"If he's saying good-bye than I'm sure that means he's accepted it." I paused. "Has Aislin removed Stephan's Mark of Immortality yet? How's that even supposed to work?"

His face sank as if he just realized there was a problem. "You know what? I have no freaking idea."

God, this was stupid. I couldn't just rely on the fact that I knew everything would work out. We still had to get there. And I didn't see the part where Aislin removed the mark and the shield.

"What are you thinking?" Laylen asked, like he knew my mind was brewing up a plan.

I tapped my fingers on the arm rest, hating to do it, but unable to think of another way. "I think I need to see one more vision."

He frowned and rested his arm across the top of the chair. "Why? I thought you weren't into that anymore?"

"I'm not." I bit at my thumb nail. "But I need to find out how Aislin takes Stephan down."

"Are you sure?" he asked. "Because I know how you've felt about visions lately."

"I'm sure." I lied down on the sofa, propping my feet onto his lap. Then I took a deep breath. "Just stay here while I go, okay?"

"Whatever you want." He patted my legs. "And I'm always here for you. You know that."

"One last Foreseer *hoorah*." I shut my eyes, picturing Stephan, the Mark of Immortality on his arm, and an invisible shield protecting his body. I let my mind go, pushing past the boundaries of the normal human mind.

And then I was there.

I was standing at the Keeper's Castle in front of the stairway. I'd been here before, but it had changed. There was ice spider webbing the ceiling and the banister. The floor was a layer of snow, the footprints of heavy traffic stamped through it. My shoes crunched as I moved to the window and drew back the curtain. There we were, Alex and I, holding hands, far across the lake. This was it. This had to be it.

Voices fluttered from the back room and I walked up the hall, my heart knocking, not because I'd see Stephan or the Death Walkers. But because this was it. This was the end.

The door was shut and I shoved it open. A cold air chilled my skin and bones. The fireplace was lifeless. The rug that spread the floor was cracked with ice as a group of Death Walkers paused, listening to Stephan rant.

"This is the day," he said, his black cloak trailing the floor as he paced with his hands behind his back. "This is the day when we all reunite."

The Death Walkers' eyes glowed, their corpse-like hands clapped as they shrieked.

"The problem is, you have failed me," he said. "You haven't given me the star. And now all I have left is a useless portal. I can't free Malefiscus. Do you know what that means?"

"But we have Death Walkers." The voice moved over my shoulder and I shuddered.

Demetrius strolled up to Stephan. He wore the same black cloak. Standing side by side, Demetrius was taller, his black hair longer, but they both carried evil in their eyes.

"We don't need Malefiscus anymore," Demetrius said. "You can create marks. You and I can rule the world."

Stephan's eyes were cold as he traced his finger along his scar. "Do you not remember what this represents? Are you forgetting where we came from?"

Demetrius flinched. "I'm not forgetting, but we don't have the star—and we can't free him without it. But we have the portal and there are enough Death Walkers to freeze over the world." He lowered his voice. "We can still do this. We can still control everything."

Stephan slammed his fist against the mantel. "He's in our blood—he's the one who started this all. Don't forget where we came from."

"And we're the ones who are going to end it." Demetrius swished back his cloak. "Years and years you've sacrificed your life protecting a world that does nothing but cause more problems. But if we do this, we can control the faeries, the witches, the vampires—everyone. Forever."

Stephan clenched his jaw. "We were supposed to free him. It was what we were born to do." He touched the scar again. "It's why we have these."

I backed against the wall as more Death Walkers packed themselves into the room, choking the air away.

"No, it's not time yet," Stephan growled at the Death Walkers. "Stop asking me that same stupid question."

Wow. He was really cracking under the pressure. I liked it.

He picked up the Sword of Immortality and ran his finger along the jagged blade. I thought he was going to stab one of them again as he strode for the nearest Death Walker.

"Breathe on this," he instructed, holding the sword in front of a Death Walker's mouth.

The Death Walker huffed and a mist puffed from its lips, blowing the Chill of Death on the blade. Then Stephan cracked it against the chair, shattering it into a thousand unusable pieces.

"No more threats," he muttered and returned to the fireplace. "Well, let's go then."

It was like an orb when it first appeared, a bright blue ball that built in the center of the room. I glanced around, wondering who was doing it. The ball moved for Stephan and he buckled back, bumping his arm against the bricks of the fireplace.

"What is that!" He barked, leaning his head back as the orb bounced for him. "Which one of you is doing this?"

"I am." Aislin materialized in the center of the ice army and she wasn't alone. Laylen towered beside her, holding her hand for support.

Stephan grinned wickedly. "Has my daughter finally come to reunite with me ... are you afraid of what's coming?"

"Nope," she said, lifting her hands and the orb raised with it. "But you should be." Then she thrust her hands forward and the orb exploded with shimmer, growing bigger and bigger, sealing around Stephan, Laylen, and herself. The Death Walkers charged, but their bodies bounced against the orb, some slamming to the floor and other's shrieking.

Demetrius stood by the door, uncaring, a true evil side-kick.

"You can't kill me." Stephan's voice simmered through the translucent wall and he showed Aislin his Mark of Immortality. "No one can."

"That's where you're wrong." She leaned forward and cupped her hand around her mouth like she was telling him a secret. "Because you're going to die today."

He laughed, the sound bubbling through the orb. "No one can kill me, especially you."

"I know." She told him confidently. "But *I* didn't say I was going to kill you, did I?" Her hands sparkled. A swirl of light, bright colors vaulted upward. "*Scutum aufero recipiam.*"

I inched toward the orb and quickly tried to memorize every word she spoke.

Nothing happened and Stephan tipped back his head, laughing wickedly. "I'm unimpressed Aislin. And a little disappointed. I would have hoped my own daughter would be able to do better than this. Guess I set my expectations too high."

"Or your arrogance too high," Laylen said and then rammed headfirst into Stephan's gut. Their bodies cracked as they hit the floor and Laylen took a swing at Stephan's face. But Stephan blocked it and reached for his boot, yanking out a knife.

I gasped, running for them, but then slid to a stop, forgetting I couldn't touch them.

Aislin rushed for them and stabbed a knife into Stephan's wrist, right in the center of his Mark of Immortality.

"Accipe bonum industria a!" Aislin faltered as she took out a small vile from her pocket and dumped the liquid on Stephan's arm, mixing it in his open wound.

Stephan elbowed Laylen and freed his hand, giving Aislin a hard slap across her cheek. She soared backward, her body knocking against the wall of the orb. Laylen sank his teeth into Stephan's arm and he retaliated with a kick to the stomach. The sphere started to spark, fading in and out.

"Laylen," Aislin screamed, crawling for him. "It's time to go! Now!"

She extended her hand and Laylen ran. But Stephan snatched hold of his leg and he tripped to the floor. He slammed Stephan's head with the heel of his boot, clawing for Aislin.

If they didn't get Stephan off, he'd transport with them. I flipped out, wondering if I was going to witness the end of one of their lives.

The orb abruptly burst with a loud thunder like a massive ocean wave rolling for land. The floor dusted with light and sparkles. One last kick from Laylen and his shoe collided with Stephan's face.

Instinctively, he jerked back, clutching his bleeding nose and lips. Laylen zipped over to Aislin and right as the Death Walkers reached the line of danger, they disappeared, going back to their lives.

"Dammit!" Stephan cried, slamming his fist against the floor. "It's gone!"

"What is?" Demetrius asked, still leaning motionless against the doorway.

Stephan's eyes burned in his direction, blood streaming down his face. "My shield!" He glanced at his arm. "And my Mark of Immortality."

"You can put it back on," he said. "So relax. It's almost time."

A ringing filled the room. Stephan retrieved his phone from his cloak. He stared at the screen before wiping the blood from his face. Then he answered it.

"What." He snarled into the receiver. A voice chattered from the other end and Stephan's face took on anger mixed with excitement. Unexpectedly he shattered the phone against the icy ground and stampeded for the door.

"What is it?" Demetrius scooted out of the way.

"Our stars waiting for us," he said and then grinned as he rushed for the outside.

Demetrius followed, a fog of ice blustering against my skin as the Death Walkers flocked after them, their yellow eyes glinting.

All of them were ready to kill Alex and me.

When the room emptied, I dropped down to the floor, my heart aching because I knew what was happening outside. I stayed there for a while. I couldn't get my legs to cooperate, so I let them lay lifelessly in front of me as I watched the ice melt and puddle in the quiet room. The air began to warm and my body thawed. I didn't want to go. But I knew I had to.

Eventually, I willed myself up and took one last glance back. I could have went to the window and seen the damage outside, but I didn't want to.

When I woke up in the living room, I was lying on the couch, my feet still on Laylen as he stared at me worriedly.

"What's wrong?" I sat up, looking around for danger lurking in the corners.

"You were ... what happened?" he asked.

"I saw what Aislin did," I said, realizing I'd been crying and I dried my tears.

"Did we win?" He looked at me with hope in his eyes "Does she remove the shield and the mark?"

I nodded. "And so do you."

He pressed his lips together, wanting to say more. His blue eyes looked brighter somehow, maybe because they weren't burden with the mark.

"Are they back yet?" I slid my legs off his lap, but he held them down. "What's wrong?"

"It's nothing." He played with his lip ring. "Would you ... could you explain to me why you have to die? Because I don't get it. If we removed his mark, then we can take him down."

"But we can't take down everything else," I told him. "Alana told me something while I was in the Afterlife. She said that everything was supposed to happen this way. And that the star had to die because if it lives, the portal will open. Malefiscus is part of the star and it connects the portal to us. He can't walk free without the blood of the rest of you guys, but the portal opening up will do enough damage to the world. And we—I can't let it open."

"I wished things were different," he mumbled, eyebrows furrowing. "I wish I could have done things different."

I didn't say anything, not completely agreeing with him. Yes, I wished most of my life had been different. But there were a few things I wouldn't change.

A bang shook the floor and I jumped to my feet, searching for a knife.

"Sophia's still down there," Laylen unnecessarily explained and pulled me back down.

"I know," I said, glancing over my shoulder at the kitchen. "Could you do me a favor?"

"Anything you want, Gemma."

"Could you free Sophia?" I asked. "After all this is over. Don't just leave her down there."

He titled his head to the side, his blue-tipped bangs falling across his forehead. "You don't hate her for what she did to you?"

I considered my answer carefully. "I don't hate her, but I don't really like her either. It's kind of strange, I guess because I know all those years her mind wasn't her own. But all the pain she caused is still fresh in my mind. She's my grandmother though, and I don't want her locked underneath the house forever. "

He fidgeted with his lip ring, perplexed in his own thoughts. "Gemma, how do you know for sure that you won't be around for this? How do you know you're going to die and Alex's isn't?"

I leaned in, lowering my voice. "Can you keep a secret?"

Chapter 44

(Alex)

Aislin dropped us in front of the house, letting out a shiver, as the cold air encircled her.

"Are you sure you want to do this?" she asked again, wrapping her arms around herself. "Because maybe there's another way. We still have a little time left."

I shook my head, opening the gate. "There's no other way, Aislin. Time's up. This is it."

"Well, I'm waiting here." She refused to step onto the sidewalk.

"That's fine." I walked for the front steps. "I'd rather do this on my own, anyway." I banged on the door, causing an eruption of howls from the neighborhood dogs. "Open up! I know you're in there."

Next door, an old woman stepped out onto her porch. "Keep it down. We don't want any nonsense."

I banged on the door again, this time louder.

"No one lives there," the old woman hissed, tying her robe. "Now leave or I'll call the police."

I shook my head, giving the door a good hard kick, and then I stomped down the stairs. I grabbed Aislin by the arm and headed down the street.

"Where are we going?" Aislin trotted to keep up.

"Just keep walking." I glanced over my shoulder at the old woman who was still watching us. I turned the corner, rounding toward the back, and hopped over the fence to the back door. "Wait here," I instructed and left Aislin on the bottom steps.

I checked the back door and the window, but both were locked. I kicked the house. "Dammit! I don't have time for this crap." I punched my fist through the window, cutting my knuckles.

"Alex!' Aislin cried over the howl of the dogs, but I was already diving headfirst through the window.

Her wail blasted my ears as soon as I hit the floor. I didn't bother taking out my knife, because I was already giving her what she wanted. I ran up the stairs and kicked down the door.

"Way to make an entrance," the Banshee sung from the windowsill, her blond hair white in the pale moonlight. "But you could have just knocked."

I took a deep breath, ready to make my offer, but she held up her hand.

"Let me guess," she said, whisking from the window. "You found your mother, but now she's trapped in the Af-

269

terlife, paying her debt until Helena will let her walk the world again."

I started to nod, but then shook my head. "But that's not why I'm here."

Her eyes were curious, her smile malicious. "Then tell me, what do you want from me?" She circled, tracing her finger across my shoulder. "I can be very giving if asked the right question."

I clutched my hands into fists, knowing this wasn't easy. But it was right. And that was all that matter. "I'm ready to make a bargain with you."

A few minutes later, I returned outside, this time using the door. Aislin was waiting for me on the steps, in the crisp snow, shivering and chattering. "Can we go now? I'm freezing my butt off."

"You should have worn a jacket," I handed her mine.

"I didn't even think about it." She put the jacket on and zipped it up. "All I could think about was you saying you're going to die."

I rubbed my hands across my face, taking in what I'd just done. I felt different, scared, but less burdened. "It'll be okay. You'll be okay."

She kicked her boots at the snow. "I know you think this is how this is supposed to work, but why can't someone save you too?"

"Because I'm not worth it." I stared at the sky. "I've lived my life, did a lot of crappy things, and now it's time to make up for it."

She sucked back the tears and sniffled. "You're not as bad as you think you are, Alex. And I think Gemma would agree with me."

I realized this was probably the last time I'd see her. When I returned home, it would be time. And even though she bugged the heck out of me most days, I'd still miss her. So I pulled her in for one last hug.

"Take care of yourself." I gave her a pat on the back.

She nodded, sobbing, just like she always did. Then she pushed back, dabbing the tears from her eyes.

"Can we make one stop before we go back to the house?" I asked. "There's something I need to get."

"Where do you want to go?" she asked. "Hopefully somewhere easy."

I shook my head. "Sorry, but this is anything but easy."

She crossed her arms defiantly. "Then I'm not going. I'm so sick of this. I just want to go back and all of us live normal lives."

"That's not going to happen," I said with honesty. "At least not for everyone."

She pressed her face into her hands. "Fine. Where to you want to go?"

My breath puffed out in front of me. "To the Keeper's Castle."

"Are you insane?" Her hands fell to her side. "You do understand that's where Stephan is, right?"

"Well, we're not going there to pay him a visit," I said. "We're going to sneak into my room."

"Why? That seems like the last thing you should be doing right now."

"You want the power for your shield spell?" The neighbor's lights clicked on and I scooted us into the shadows. "You remember how Gemma and I use to steal crap from Stephan all the time, just to piss him off."

"Yeah, I always thought you guys were stupid." She laughed her eyes wide as she stared off into space.

"Not stupid," I said. "Smart. I have quite the collection hidden in my room."

"I'm surprised you didn't give it all back to him," she said. "I mean, after she left you seemed to just do what he asked."

I motioned my hand, stirring the falling snow. "Everything happens for a reason. Now can we go? We're running low on time."

She glanced at the sky and nodded. Then she chanted under her breath as the snow sped us away.

When we hit my bedroom floor, both our feet slipped out from under us. I braced myself with the bedpost but Aislin fell to the floor, her elbow cracking against the ice.

My eyes did a quick scan of the room, making sure it was empty. There was ice everywhere, coating the walls and the floor. Icicles hung from the ceiling.

Aislin winced, cupping her elbow as she sat up. "What? Are they just living here now? He's really lost it, hasn't he?"

"I don't think he ever had anything to lose." I stood, getting my balance and headed for the trapdoor. But it was frozen shut by ice. "You got your knife on you?"

"Yeah." She regained her steadiness with her hands extended to the side. "Why?"

"Because we're going to have to chip some ice away to get to the stuff."

She took her knife out of her snow boot, knelt down, and stabbed at the ice.

"Quietly." I sat down with my knife in my hand and shaved a layer of ice away. Aislin followed my lead and it seemed like we worked for hours, before we removed enough that I could snap the door open. Finally I glided inside, remembering the time Gemma and I hid in the space. It was one of the most unbearable moments of my life; hours seemed like days and I was surprised we even made it out alive.

Hidden at the farthest wall was a bag. I snatched it up, rolled over, and heaved myself back up. Aislin grabbed it from me and untied it.

Her eyes sparkled. "Holy crap." She blinked at me. "How did you get all this?"

Inside the bag were many things that contained a lot of power; The Flower of Malina, The Box of Aurora, The Dust of The Burning Bridge. To me, it had always been a bunch of useless stuff. But maybe Aislin could use the power for her spell.

"Dad's always been power crazy," I said. "I just hope they'll work for you."

"So do I," she said enthusiastically. "But there's only one way to find out for sure."

We scared them with our sudden appearance in the middle of the living room.

Gemma hopped to her feet, her violet eyes stormy and anxious. "Where were you?" She tried to sound calm, but failed.

"I had something to do before we headed to the lake." My hands longed to touch her, like they did last night.

She bit at her lip, her expression loosening from wrath to uncertainty. "So where did you go?"

"Aislin and I just wanted to say our good-byes." I glanced at Aislin, warning her not to say anything.

Aislin sighed and flopped down on the sofa dramatically. "This is the most depressing day ever."

Gemma stared at Aislin for a second, like she sensed something was up. "So you're okay with this?" She turned her head to me. "You're totally on board with this plan now?"

274

I pressed my lips together, giving a slow nod. "If it means saving the world ... then yeah."

She struggled not to cry as she took everything in. "Aislin, I need you to do something."

"What's up?" Aislin twirled her hair around her finger, her foot tapping against the floor as she tried to act normal.

"I found out how you got the shield spell and mark off Stephan," she said, absentmindedly touching the Foreseer mark on the back of her neck.

"You went into another vision?" I asked. "Gemma, I—"

"There's no point in arguing." She cut me off. "Now let me tell her what she needs to do."

I wondered if this was how people felt when they went into battle. If their hearts drummed, their insides shook, and their minds begged them not to go.

I'd spent so much time not really getting to know the good things in life. I'd carried my father's negative energy, but I was finally shedding it.

"So we have to go to the Castle?" Aislin asked, eyes wide as she hugged the bag. "And all of them will be there."

"You'll be fine," Gemma said as I sat down on the armrest behind her, feeling the static, but not caring anymore. "I've seen it with my own eyes."

Aislin reached for her herb box on the table. "Well, let's get going, I guess."

"Don't you still need more power?" Laylen leaned forward and picked up a baggy.

Aislin took it from his fingers and handed him the bag we'd picked up. "Look inside."

Laylen gave her a warily look, untied the bag, and peered in. "Where did you get this?"

"Alex had it," she said. "He used to steal all kinds of stuff from Stephan when he was a kid."

"When *we* were kids." I brushed Gemma's hair with my fingers, letting her know I meant her.

She tipped her head back and I could tell by her violet eyes she still couldn't remember.

Aislin opened her spell book and flipped through the pages until she landed on one titled: Potentia Aufero. "Everybody ready for this?" she asked and no one spoke a word. "Okay then." She stretched her hands and dumped the bag onto the table. Gemma gasped as the strange items piled out. "Pretty amazing, huh?" Then Aislin's face grew serious as she hovered her hand over the pile. "*Ego hanc vim solummodo bonum. Hoc opus auxilium. Da me potestatem.*"

A red diamond, shaped like a bleeding heart, flickered first. Then all the others harmonized, producing a collection of flaring colors so intense it was hard to look at it. But all four of us couldn't look away, watching as the colors looped for Aislin, slipping across her hands and making her skin blaze bright. She sucked in a breath and her head

276

rolled back. "It's wonderful," she breathed, staring at her hands. "Like ..."

"Electricity," Gemma said quietly.

Aislin nodded. "Is this how you guys feel all the time?"

Gemma didn't reply, staring out the window, the sun breaking against the horizon and lighting up the world. "Do you think it's time?" she asked to no one in particular "Or do you think we need to wait until later today."

"It's December 21st," I said. "I'm sure that's all that matters." I paused. "Is that it? Do you have everything for your spell?"

"Yeah, I have more than enough." She was still beaming over her new power.

"Then I guess we should all get going," Gemma said, the electricity picking up with her anxiousness.

We all sat there, afraid to move. It was a moment of silence that could be felt around the world, as if time actually stopped for a brief second to take it all in.

Aislin stood first and Laylen followed her lead. "Do we go all at once?" Laylen asked.

"Alex and I were outside in the vision, so yeah, I think we go all at once." Gemma trailed over to the corner armoire and took a cellphone out of the drawer.

"Where did you get that?" I asked.

"We found it in the house after you left. I think it was Sophia's." She opened it and held the power button down. "We kept it around in case of an emergency."

"And this is an emergency?" I took the phone from her as it clicked on.

"It's how we're going to bring Stephan out of the house," she replied, staring off into emptiness.

"With a phone?" I cocked an eyebrow and then shrugged, stuffing the phone into my pocket. "You ready?"

She nodded, squeezing her eyes tight as if she were trying to crush this moment from her mind. She began to cry as Laylen stood up and hugged her tight.

"Bye," she whispered, her hands unsteady as she clutched onto him for dear life. "And remember what I said."

Laylen's expression was raw pain. But when they broke away from each other, the look was gone. Gemma turned to Aislin, not sure what to do. But I knew what would happen, because Aislin was Aislin. She grabbed Gemma, crying like she always did, even though she knew the outcome.

Gemma looked awkward with the whole thing, but gave it her best. Aislin finally released her and Gemma took my hand, our fingers intertwining, sparks going crazy, begging us not to touch. But we didn't care anymore. Our time together was up. The star would soon be dead. And the world would move on.

"Ready for this?" she asked.

"I've been ready for this for forever."

She didn't catch my meaning, grasping onto my hand, and closing her eyes.

But I meant what I'd said. I had been waiting for this day forever.

Because today was the day I was finally going to save her.

Chapter 45

(Gemma)

Saying good-bye to Laylen was the second hardest thing I ever had to do. The first was just around the corner. And that was saying goodbye to Alex.

I Foreseed us to the edge of the lake, right on the shore, our backs to the grey-stoned Keeper's Castle. I wondered if the Water Faeries were down there, watching us from beneath the water, wishing we'd fall in so they could torture us.

Everything seemed clear now; clearer than it had ever been for me. My head had always been so packed with thoughts and worries. But they were all gone now. The answers were right in front of me.

Well, almost.

I turned in a circle. "I don't think we're in the right spot."

He gazed around, scratching his head. "Where are we supposed to be then?"

I pointed at the trees. "Well, all of them came from there, but right now they're in the castle."

He kicked a rock into the lake and the water rippled. "We should have had you see the whole vision then."

"No, we shouldn't have." My eyes took in the trees. Then I shut my eyes and breathed in the air. "You feel that ...." My eyes opened. "The Death Walkers."

"That was really creepy," he said, forcing a light tone. "It's like you smelled them or something."

"No, I just felt the cold air."

My eyes lingered on the castle, the electricity warming up, preparing itself for the end. The grass was kissed with morning dew, the sun barely breaking.

He stared at the other side of the lake and then he took off, dragging me with him.

"What are you doing?" I stammered, tripping over rocks and twigs.

"Making this right." He dodged us around a large tree. "You said they came from the trees. So we will see them coming and have enough time."

We ran by our hideout, the violet bush flitting away from my sight as we raced farther into the forest. I stamped the picture in my head, wanting to take it with me forever: two kids, pressing hands tightly, promising to be together forever.

Little did they understand that their time would be short and precious. That their forever was merely a glitch in time.

We walked the half circle around the lake, breaking from the forest edge and out into the open. The lake stretched between us and the castle.

"This work?" He pointed at the castle. "We can see when they're coming."

"I think so." I memorized the trees, the water, the sun hiding behind the clouds.

He took the phone out of his pocket. "What did I say when I called?"

"I don't know." I shrugged. "I guess that's up to you."

He dialed the number and put the phone to his ear. It rang and rang and rang and then I heard the muffled "what."

"Look out your window." He paused, raising his hand and flipping his father off. "If you want us, come get us asshole." Then he snapped the phone shut.

"That was your final words to him?" I questioned, my breath and heart erratic.

He chucked the phone into the lake. "Yep, that's all I had to say."

Suddenly everything moved fast like flickers of light-ning bolts flashing across the sky. They barreled out the front door of the castle, their cloaks blowing behind them as they froze the land over.

He clutched onto my hand. "Breathe, Gemma."

I sucked in a breath as the sounds of ice and twigs and wind blew around us. Alex said something to me, but his words were just whispers of a language I would soon forget. Tears filled my eyes, but I couldn't take them off the trees, frozen with icicles, as they marched closer and closer, irreversibly breaking free from the shade of the forest. It was Stephan's eyes I saw first, cold and deadly, and then Alex regained my focus.

"It will be alright," he whispered and then he kissed me, like I was the only thing left on this world, like he could finally breathe for the very first time. Like we were one. And I finally realized something, all on my own, without the help of the prickle.

"I love you." My words carried away in the wind. I didn't say it because he was perfect or because every time I was with him it was magical. Nothing was perfect and I understood that. I said it because I was standing here in death and there was no one else I wanted beside me.

"I love you," he whispered back. "Always have. Always will. Forever."

And those were the magic words, the ones that burned the light free. It was the words that emptied us, but freed us at the same time, along with the star. Its energy smoldered brightly for the very last time and swallowed us with it.

I saw everything that had been and would never be. I saw my past and a future I would never know. Every emotion I ever felt flashed through me at once: hurt, happiness, pain, love. And then my body sank as my life slipped away and I became one with the earth. The star had expired, saving the world, not ending it. But taking my soul with it.

But I would never forget him. No matter what happened.

Because we were bonded together.

Forever.

Chapter 46
(Gemma)

Death wasn't bad. Death was warm and bright and weightless, like air. It was like I'd soared off to the sun, away from my pain, forgetting everything.

Until I heard the Banshee wail and I opened my eyes.

Then I remembered the bargain I made with Helena. I promised her my soul, handing it to her on a silver platter. To her, it was the best kind of soul. In exchange, Alex would live, continuing on with his life, free from his father and the star.

It might have seemed like a crazy choice, but once Helena spoke it, I knew there wasn't a choice left. When faced with the option to save everyone and only have to let myself go, I had to pick death. Otherwise I'd never have been able to live with myself.

"And so we meet again." Helena's old tattered body was perched in her throne. Her silver eyes were eager, happy to collect my soul.

"And so we do," I said, stepping onto the red podium, no longer afraid. What was done was done. "So what do I do now? Become your slave? Turn into one of your mummies?"

Her lip twitched at my tone. "You do whatever I want you to do." Then she clapped her hands. "In fact I have the perfect place for you. You will live inside my ring, close by, where I can always feed off your power."

"My power's dead." I spat. "There's nothing left inside me."

"You sound very ungrateful." She stood to her feet, her twiggy legs wobbling her toward me. "Must I remind you that this was your choice—you wanted this."

"It was never a choice." I got in her face, not angry, not calm, not anything. "I did what I had to do."

She tipped back her crinkled head. "You're a stupid little girl. And I'm going to eat you up." She paused with a clever look in her silver eyes. "I think I have a better place for you." Then she opened her hollow mouth, her breath stinking of a corpse. "You can live inside me."

I stood inert as she breathed me in. I didn't feel like working up a fight. I felt like my old self, empty and numb—emotionless. I shut my eyes, preparing for my real end, hoping I could go into the dark forever.

"Helena."

My eyes snapped open. Behind the throne was Annabella. Her white lily hair blew like fire. Her red lips were pursed, and her silver eyes narrowed.

"Let her go," Annabella said. "She's not yours to take."

Helena whirled, her crippled body popping as she stormed for Annabella. "This doesn't concern you."

Annabella stepped slowly onto the podium and swished her black dress to the side. As they stood in front of each other, Helena was much smaller than Annabella.

"You feel that," Annabella whispered. "You can't take her soul because it belongs to someone else."

"She gave it to me!" Helena roared, stomping her foot. "I can take it!"

"You've always been so greedy," Annabella said. "No wonder mother liked you less."

Helena's hands moved for Annabella's throat. "I hate you!"

Annabella seized her hands, trapping her in place. "Her soul is connected to another. You can't have it, even if you made a bargain with her. You have no right and if I have to, I'll bring down mother to talk to you."

Helena kicked and yanked, like a child. "We had a bargain! We had a bargain!"

Annabella's eyes fired ferociously. "I'm going to take her now. She's not staying." Then she let Helena go.

Helena sank to the floor, her head falling into her hands as she wailed.

Annabella extended her hand. "Come with me, Gemma."

Given the two choices, I took Annabella's hand. "Where are we going?"

She led me to the back of the throne and a light curtained around us. "To your mother."

She carried us away in a light full of essence and warmth and landed us underneath the cape of the willow tree. Then Annabella was no longer there. The branches danced around my mother and me as we faced each other, unblinking.

"Mom." I threw my arms around her neck and sobbed. "I thought I'd never see you again."

She smoothed my hair. "Shhh ... everything's going to be okay." She let me have a moment, let my tears soak her shirt. Then she pulled me away so she could look at me. "Do you know why you're here?"

I wiped my eyes with the back of my hand and sniffed. "Because I crossed over. I'm essence now."

She shook her head, her dark hair twirling in the wind. "You're here because of who you are."

"Who am I?" I asked. "This is all so confusing."

"You're my daughter, brave and loving. Both are wonderful gifts."

"I think you're wrong." I frowned. "Those don't sound like me at all."

She smiled delicately. "But they are, Gemma. They really are."

"Is that why I was freed from Helena?" I tucked my hair behind my ears. "Because I sacrificed my life."

She walked for the middle of the tree, her blue dress whipping behind her. "You're here because everything happens for a reason. You're here because both of you made the sacrifice."

"I'm not sure I understand." I followed her. "Both of us made the sacrifice. Did Alex die too?"

She quickly shook her head. "You're here because you carry the soul of another, which means Helena can't make a bargain with just you. She'd also have to make one with Alex. No one can own either of your souls without the other."

"So I'm an essence?" I turned over my arms, wondering if I was going to turn into an orb.

"Is that what you want?" Her blue eyes were pressing. "Do you want to be here?"

"Do I have another choice?"

She sat down on the grass. "If you choose to stay here with me you can. But if you choose to leave, you can go back to your life."

"My life," I whispered, a gentle breeze kissing at my cheeks.

"If you want."

I sat down on the ground beside her and plucked at the grass, thinking about my life. "But why is Annabella letting me go? Why doesn't she keep me?"

"Because she can let you go," my mother said. "She can either let you go or take you both. You and Alex are bonded—take one, they have to take you both."

We're bonded together forever. "But why not just take us both?"

"I know this is hard for you to understand, but not everything is evil." She picked a violet flower from the ground and spun it in her fingers. "What you did to save the lives of everyone else that was the very essence of good. You need to understand that everything isn't evil in the world. There is also good."

"And Annabella's good?" I let go of the pieces of grass and watched them blow into the garden full of lilies, roses, and vines twisting from the trees.

"Annabella is what she chooses to be," she said. "Just like you can."

I swallowed hard, letting it sink in. "I didn't expect this. I thought I became a Lost Soul."

"I know. And that's why you're one of the good ones. You went into this blind." She paused, handing me the violet flower. "So what will it be, Gemma? Do you choose life? Or death?"

I stared at the flower as it rested in the palm of my hand. "What about you?"

"I'm right where I belong," she said. "It's you that needs a place."

"I don't think I can leave you," I muttered. "Knowing I'll never see you again. You took your own life to save me. Why don't you get a choice?"

"We'll see each other again." She squeezed my hand. "This isn't good-bye forever."

I thought about life, about the pain I'd been through. But the tiniest moments—the stolen kisses, the whispered words, the possibilities—helped me to choose. I released the flower and let the wind carry it away to the unknown. "I want to go back."

White and red flower petals blew through the air as she nodded and stood to her feet, brushing the grass off her dress. "One last good-bye before you go."

I hugged her with all I had in me, not wanting to let go, but knowing I had to. When I backed away, she was gone and Annabella stepped out from behind the tree.

"You choose life?" She asked. "Is that your final decision?"

I nodded. "I choose life."

Chapter 47

(Alex)

The light was warm as it took me away. I could feel her pulse racing to the very end. She was terrified of her death and I wanted to tell her that it was okay—that she wouldn't die. But I couldn't.

When I opened my eyes, I was lying on the floor of the burnt house in Iceland. The cry of the Banshee was nails to my ears. I pushed to my feet, searching for her, wanting to get this over with.

She was curled in the corner, in her hag form, her skin wrinkled and tattered. Her thin hair hung in her eyes and she showed me her yellow teeth as she smiled. "I've been waiting for you."

I stuffed my hands in my pockets. "Have you? I'm so thrilled."

She crept to her feet. "I can't believe I have you. I've waited forever to get my hands on a soul like yours. Not many humans like to throw theirs away so carelessly."

"It wasn't careless," I replied, thinking of Gemma. Had she woken up and realized she was still alive?

She trialed her fingernails along my shoulder and then ran her hands through my hair. "It seems careless if you ask me—throwing your soul away, all to save the life of a human girl."

I swatted her hand away. "First off, stay the hell away from me. Just because you own my soul doesn't mean you can put your gross, wrinkly hands on me."

She snarled and then smiled wickedly. "You're mine now and I'll do whatever I want with you." Then she danced around, shifting into her other form. Her hair thickened and her skin smoothed over. "There. Is that better for you?" She reached for me again.

I shoved her back. "I said don't touch me."

"You can be bitter all you want," she replied. "But eventually I'll break you."

I was already broken. "So what's next? Do you make me your slave? Send me to the Afterlife? Tell me what your great plan is."

She traced her hands along the burnt walls and pieces crumbled to the floor. "You're very ungrateful. When you came here asking me to take your soul in return for freeing the girls, I thought I was doing you a favor."

"You were." I gritted my teeth. "But it doesn't mean I hate you any less."

She dropped her hand, smacking her lips. "Free souls are hard to find. Even Helena herself would kill for one.

The power yours will give me can help me take her down."

"So that's your big plan," I said, snorting a laugh. "You take my soul and try to take down the Queen of the Afterlife. Great plan. You really must be a true genius."

She lunged for me, wringing my neck and pinning me against the wall. And I let her because I had no fight left in me.

"Defend yourself," she growled. "Or it won't be any fun."

"Let him go." The voice chilled the air, but warmed my skin.

The Banshee let me go, her lips trembling as she turned for the doorway. A woman with white hair, blood red lips, and silver eyes stood in her path.

The Banshee bowed her head. "I'm sorry Annabella. But he gave me his soul."

"His soul wasn't his to give." Annabella walked into the room, glancing around at the charred walls. "So this is what the entrance of the Afterlife has come to. Looks like things have taken a turn for the worse."

"They have," the Banshee said excitedly. "Perhaps soon, Helena will no longer rule."

Annabella shoved her to the floor. "I may not like my sister. But to utter such words about her in my presence is dishonorable."

The Banshee wept and curled into a ball. "I'm so sorry."

Annabella ignored her, her silvery eyes landing on me. "So this is what you offered in exchange for the freedom of her soul." She pulled a disgusted face at the room. "Very brave of you."

"You're the Queen of the Afterlife's sister?" I asked. "So that makes you the—"

"It makes me nothing," she said. "I choose to be whatever I am. But if you want to know what I reign over, it's the essences."

I grew worried that something had gone wrong. "Why are you here?"

She eyed me over. "I think what you really want to ask is if she's okay—if she lived because of your sacrifice?"

"Is she?" I asked. "Is she still alive?"

She pressed her lips together and her gaze was heavy. "Tell me, why did you do it?"

"Because she was my other half," I said. "And because I love her."

"Other half?" she considered this with curiosity. "It's a beautiful concept to me, and maybe that's why I'm doing this. It's an amazing gift for two humans to bond themselves together as tight as you have."

"What are you doing?" My eyes darted to the Banshee as she crawled for Annabella.

"Please don't take him from me," she begged. "I need him."

"So you can try and take Helena's place." She laughed. "That'll never happen." Then she whirled her

295

back on me. "Make sure you live your life the way you want. Second chances are precious and don't come around often."

Before I could ask her what she meant, I was sucked away into blackness.

Chapter 48
(Gemma)

The first thing I saw when I opened my eyes was the sky. It was crystal blue, the clearest I'd ever seen it. I could hear rippling water, the song of the wind, the breaths of the birds and animals.

I could hear life.

His hand was still in mine, but his skin was cold. I quickly sat up and leaned over him. "Alex, can you hear me?" He lay motionless and I shook him gently. "Alex, wake up."

But he didn't stir. I put my hand on his chest. He wasn't breathing. I sucked back my tears. "But you weren't supposed to die."

And then all at once his eyes opened and it was like every ounce of worry and pain elevated from my body. "Oh my God." I sighed back, resting my hands against the grass.

He sat up and clutched his head. "What the heck happened?"

"We died," I said. "But everything's okay now."

He arched his eyebrow at me. "You died? But you weren't supposed to."

"When I was in the Afterlife." I shielded my eyes from the sun. "I told Helena I would give her my soul when I died, in exchange for your life."

He suppressed a smile.

"What's so funny?" I asked.

"Nothing, it's just that I made the same promise with a Banshee." He lay on the grass, shaking his head and smiling. "God, we really are bonded together. We even made the same self-sacrificing choice." Then he turned serious. "But why are we here? Alive?"

I traced the scar on my palm. "Because our souls are connected. If they take one, they take us both."

He sat up, pressing his hand into mine. "Then why not take us both?"

"Because good does exist apparently."

"It was the promise," he said, finally explaining. "When we made the Forever Promise, our souls mix with each other."

"Did you ..." I hesitated. "Did you know that when you did it?"

He tangled our fingers, pressing back an amused grin. "I told you, I know everything."

I shook my head, but smiled. And it was easy like air. "Do you feel that?"

"Feel what?"

"Exactly."

The electricity was gone. Even though it had brought intensity, it had also brought pain. And I was glad to see it go.

We sat, staring at the water, stained with the ashes of the evil that eventually would drift away. The peaceful moment was interrupted when my wrist began to burn. At first I didn't look, not wanting to move and shatter the calm bubble that had built around us. But the pain became too intense and I tore my eyes from the water and turned my arm over. Tattooing my wrist was a simple outline of a star. I traced the lines with my fingers, curious what it was. Then Alex put his wrist next to mine and I understood.

"Is it ours?" I asked.

He pressed his lips together and smiled. "I think it is."

As the sun slipped away behind the mountains and the stars awoke, he touched his lips to mine. And we stayed that way for as long as we wanted.

No more rush, no more worry. We had all the time in the world.

Chapter 49
(Gemma)

"She was a mean little thing," I pulled a face. "And I didn't expect her to be so … so …"

"Short?" Laylen finished for me and then laughed. "What did you think? That faeries had to be tall or something?" He nudged my shoulder.

I stuck out my tongue. "No, but I expected the Empress of the Faerie realm to be tall." I ducked underneath a branch as we made our way back. "And what were those little creatures? One of them tried to bite me."

"Those were sprites." Aislin shoved through a screen of vines. "They're mean!"

"Did you know you'll turn into one if they bite you," he said and I couldn't tell if he was joking.

"I still can't believe Aleesa didn't want to come back." I hopped over a tree trunk that extended across the path.

"I'm not," Laylen said. "She was always a little off. She'll fit right in."

I heard the pitter-patter of tiny footsteps and glanced back just in time to see a sprite, with its wings out, running at an impressive speed for such tiny legs. It leapt for my ankle and I drop kicked it like a soccer ball. It flew through the air and landed far back in the trees with a thud.

"Wow, she's mean," Aislin kidded.

"Well, I don't want to turn into one of them," I said.

Laylen laughed, shaking his head. "You do realize I was kidding about that."

I pulled a face and sped up, leaving the two of them behind, anxious to get back to the castle. As I broke through the faerie realm and stepped out onto the land that fronted the Keeper's castle, my heart leapt with excitement.

When I'd decided to go with them, I didn't realize what I was getting myself into. And it turned out to be a waste of a trip anyway.

I headed inside, glad to be back to the normal world. Even though we weren't connected by the electricity anymore, I could still sense where he was and I walked straight to the back room.

He was with Sophia, who wasn't all that bad, once the evil had left her. Still, I struggled sometimes to be around her because it reminded me of the past.

The two of them were huddled over a book, in front of the fireplace, talking about something.

His eyes found mine and he smiled in a way that made my skin warm with my own heat.

"I'll be right back," Sophia said and then she saw me and smiled. "You guys made it back okay?"

"Yeah, Aislin and Laylen are coming." I nodded at the window.

"Good. I'm glad you're okay." She stood in front of me awkwardly. She acted like she wanted to say more, but smiled instead and walked out the door.

She did that a lot. Perhaps one day she'd finally be able say what was on her mind.

Alex closed the book and walked across the room, carrying something in his hands.

"Did you two find out anything about how to free a Foreseer from the Room of Forbidden?" I asked.

"Maybe," he answered. "We have to do a little bit more research, but there might be a way to free your dad … although, it'll be kind of difficult."

"We saved the world," I said. "So I'm sure we can do it, whatever it is."

"I'm sure we can." He laughed and then paused. "So did you guys get everything taken care of?"

I shook my head. "Nope. Not even close."

He laughed softly, putting his hand on my hip. "Isn't that always the case?"

I let out a sigh. "Aleesa didn't want to come back. I guess she liked it there. But the Empress—I mean Luna, still thinks Aislin owes her the spell."

He slid his hand up my back and hooked something around my neck.

I stared down at my violet-stoned locket. "Where did you get this?"

He winked at me. "Where you lost it."

I clasped the heart-shaped pendant in my hand, forcing the tears back as I thought of my mother. "But how did you get it back from them?"

He arched an eyebrow. "You think two witches scare me?"

I shook my head, wondering what had really happened.

"So what's Aislin going to do?" He asked. "With the spell? She's not going to do it is she?"

I shrugged. "She told the Empress she'd work on it."

"Work on it." He sketched his finger down my cheek. "She's powerful enough to do the spell on her own."

"Yeah, but Luna doesn't know that." I frowned, remembering the faerie realm. I always thought Nicholas was bad, but he definitely was the more tolerable of the faerie breed. I had seen him once since it all happened and wasn't surprised he had returned to being his trickster self. "And I still don't get why Aleesa wanted to stay there. I mean, I know she thinks she likes it, but that place was just weird."

"Aleesa's weird." He smiled, moving his lips for mine. "And what does it matter if she's happy."

"You're right," I said and met him the rest of the way, pressing my lips to his.

We kissed, our souls beating as one. Always and forever.

Jessica Sorensen lives with her husband and three kids in the snowy mountains of Wyoming, where she spends most of her time reading, wring, and hanging out with her family.

Other books by Jessica Sorensen:
The Fallen Star (Fallen Star Series, Book 1)
The Underworld (Fallen Star Series, Book 2)
The Vision (Fallen Star Series, Book3)

Connect with me online:
http://jessicasorensensblog.blogspot.com/
http://www.facebook.com/pages/Jessica-Sorensen/165335743524509
https://twitter.com/#!/jessFallenStar

21858735R00178

Made in the USA
Lexington, KY
01 April 2013